The Missing Will

The Amish Millionaire
PART 4 OF 6

Wanda E. Brunstetter
& Jean Brunstetter

The Missing Will

SHILOH RUN PRESS
An Imprint of Barbour Publishing, Inc.

Print ISBN 978-1-63409-206-7

eBook Editions:
Adobe Digital Edition (.epub) 978-1-63409-854-0
Kindle and MobiPocket Edition (.prc) 978-1-63409-857-1

All scripture quotations are taken from the King James Version of the Bible.

This book is a work of fiction. Names, characters, places, and incidents are either products of the author's imagination or used fictitiously. Any similarity to actual people, organizations, and/or events is purely coincidental.

Cover design: Müllerhaus Publishing Arts Inc., www.mullerhaus.net
Cover model photography: Richard Brunstetter III: RIII Studios
Cover photography: Doyle Yoder

Published by Shiloh Run Press, an imprint of Barbour Publishing, Inc., P.O. Box 719, Uhrichsville, Ohio 44683, www.shilohrunpress.com

Our mission is to publish and distribute inspirational products offering exceptional value and biblical encouragement to the masses.

Printed in the United States of America.

Chapter 1

Akron, Ohio

Blinking against tears threatening to spill over, Kristi struggled to keep her focus on the road. Breaking up with Joel had been one of the hardest things she'd ever done. But it was the right decision. Her fingers turned white as she gripped the steering wheel. *I can't believe all the lies he's told me.*

Nothing about Joel made sense anymore. She'd been blinded by his good looks and charm. *I should have listened to Mom.* Kristi still didn't understand the reason he'd kept his Amish heritage from her for so long or why he'd taken money from their joint account without telling her. If he hadn't foolishly used money he'd earned on a job to buy a classic car he didn't need, Joel wouldn't be in a financial bind.

Kristi reflected on how desperate he'd seemed when he asked his sister Elsie about the will on the day of his father's funeral. Joel had acted selfishly and unfeelingly. She couldn't picture herself asking about her parents' will so soon after one of them had passed away. Was Joel really that desperate for money?

Her throat constricted as she changed lanes. "For the love of money is the root of all evil," she murmured, quoting 1 Timothy 6:10. She reflected on 1 Timothy 6:7, as well: "For we brought nothing into this world, and it is certain we can carry nothing out." Kristi had committed those two verses to memory when she'd attended a Bible study on money management a few years ago. *Too bad I didn't think to quote those scriptures to Joel when he told me how desperate he was for money. If he needed funds for a good cause, that would be one thing, but to waste it on a car he could certainly live without was foolish.*

The longer Kristi thought about things, the more she wanted to pull to the side of the road and break down in tears. It would probably do her good to go for a run to release some tension, but right now she needed a listening ear. Turning at the next road, Kristi headed for her parents' house. She hoped they were home.

Farmerstown, Ohio

"Are you okay?" Arlene's husband, Larry, looked at her with concern. "You were quiet on the buggy ride home from church, and since we've gotten here, all you've done is sit and stare out the kitchen window."

Arlene sighed as she clutched her damp handkerchief. "I miss my *daed*, Larry. Remember how almost every Sunday when his district didn't have church, he would attend service with us? Looking at the men's side this morning and not seeing him there didn't seem right." Tears pooled in her eyes. "Then the three of us always came here for a meal, and afterward we'd visit, sing, or play games."

Larry sat beside Arlene and placed his hand on her shoulder. "I'm here for you, no matter what. We all miss your daed, but it's been the hardest for you, Elsie, and Doris."

She sniffed, raising her handkerchief to wipe tears from her eyes. "The *kinner* miss him, too. Dad loved our children, and they looked forward to spending time with him after church." She pointed to the birdhouse on a post outside the kitchen window. "Every time I look at that, I'll think of Dad and be glad Doris found it."

"When the lightning struck your daed's tree house, it's amazing everything in and around the tree didn't burn to a crisp."

She lowered her arm and turned toward him. "It's a shame Doris didn't find four birdhouses on the ground beneath the tree—then Joel could have had one, too."

"Do you think he would have wanted a birdhouse?" Larry's brows furrowed. "From what I can tell, the only thing your *bruder* wants is your daed's money."

Arlene swallowed hard, remembering how Joel had acted after the funeral dinner. When he'd asked about Dad's will, everyone in the room became upset. "We do need to find the document. It's the only way we'll know how he wanted things divided among us. I only hope when Joel comes around here again he won't create another scene."

"If he does, one of us will set him straight."

With shoulders slumped and head down, their youngest son, Scott, shuffled into the room.

"What's wrong, Son? You look *umgerennt*." When Scott looked up, Larry motioned for him to come over to them.

Scott stepped up to the table. "I ain't upset. I'm *bedauerlich*."

Arlene slipped her arm around him. "Why are you sad? Do you miss your *grossdaadi*?"

"*Jah*. Not only that, but I won't get to watch Peaches climb the ladder to Grandpa's tree house."

Arlene tipped her head. "Peaches?"

"You know—she's Henry Raber's *hund*. Henry said Peaches likes to climb. Since the tree house is gone now, me and Doug won't get to see her do it." Scott kicked the floor with the toe of his shoe and lowered his gaze. "Won't get to go up there and enjoy the view with Grandpa, neither."

"I'm sorry, Son." Larry pulled the boy into a hug. "Your *mamm* and I know you miss your grossdaadi, as we all do, but we have lots of fond memories of him."

Larry was right, but Arlene couldn't stop thinking about their children having lost their grandfather, whom they all loved and respected. She had hoped he would see them grow up, get married, and have kids of their own. It was hard to accept the changes in life that she couldn't control and were not what she'd planned.

"Why don't we gather the rest of the family together in the living room? We can sing some of our favorite songs for a while," she suggested.

"It won't be the same without Grandpa here, playin' his harmonica." Scott frowned. "Guess I'll never learn to play the mouth harp now, neither."

"Maybe your uncle Joel can teach you." Larry ruffled the top of Scott's thick brown hair. "As I recall, he's pretty good at playing the harmonica."

I doubt that's ever going to happen. Joel doesn't seem to care about anyone but himself. Arlene made sure not to voice her thoughts. Even though she was upset with her brother, the last thing she wanted to do was turn any of her children against him.

"Say, I have an idea." She rose from her chair. "After we sing awhile, I'll fix some snacks."

"Can we make popcorn?" Scott's eyes brightened a bit.

She nodded. "Jah, we'll do that."

"How about hot chocolate and marshmallows to go with it?" Larry smacked his lips. "That always tastes good with popcorn."

"We can have some of those peanut butter *kichlin* in the cookie jar, too." Arlene gave her son's arm a tender squeeze. "Now why don't you go let your brother and sisters know what our plans are for the rest of the afternoon?"

"Okay, Mom." Scott grinned at his parents and hurried from the room.

Larry looked over at Arlene and smiled. "It's nice to see our boy smiling again."

"Jah. A little joy is something we all need right now."

Akron

Kristi felt relieved when she pulled up to her parents' house and saw their car parked in the driveway. She was desperate to talk to someone right now—someone who would understand and offer support.

She'd no more than stepped onto the porch, when the front door swung open. "This is a surprise. I thought you and Joel went on a picnic today." Mom stood in the doorway, drying her hands on a towel.

"We did, but we ended it early, so I. . .I decided to come here."

"Are you all right?" Mom asked as she let Kristi into the house. "Your eyes are red. Have you been crying?"

Kristi looked at her shoes, struggling to keep her emotions in check. "You don't have to worry about fixing lunch for us next Sunday, because Joel and I won't be coming."

"How come?"

"Is Dad here? I'd like him to hear this, too."

"He's in the living room, reading the newspaper." Mom gestured in that direction. "Let's go in, and you can tell us all about it."

After Kristi took a seat on the couch between her parents, she told them everything that had been discussed at the picnic and explained how Joel had taken money from their account without her knowledge.

"You need to pull out the rest of the money and close that account before every penny is gone." Dad's expression was somber.

Kristi cupped her cheeks in her hands. "Oh, you're right. I'll take care of it first thing tomorrow morning." Since Joel had taken over half of the money they'd saved, she was certainly entitled to what was left.

Dad's eyebrows furrowed, and he gave a quick snort. "I can't understand why he'd do something like that. Didn't he realize what it would do to your relationship?" He slapped the folded newspaper on the coffee table. "I'm disappointed in him. Joel is obviously not the man I thought he was."

Kristi dabbed at the tears dribbling down her cheeks. "I think. . .Joel's so caught up with his need for money. . ." Her voice broke on a sob. "He's not thinking of anything but himself."

To her surprise, instead of Mom saying something negative or reminding her of what the Bible said about being unequally yoked with an unbeliever, she pulled Kristi into her arms. "I know you must be hurting right now, but perhaps in time you'll find someone else—someone better for you."

Kristi sniffed against Mom's shoulder, returning the hug. "I. . .I can't even think about that right now."

"And you shouldn't, either." Dad reached

over and took Kristi's hand. "You need time to work through your pain and heal. Always remember, your mom and I are here for you."

"That's right," Mom agreed. "If you need to talk or want someone to pray with you, come by anytime or give us a call."

"Thanks. I will." As Kristi reached into her purse for a tissue, her cell phone rang. Seeing it was Joel, she let her voice mail answer the call.

Joel held his cell phone up to his ear and grimaced when he heard Kristi's voice mail pick up. It was the fourth time he'd tried to call since she'd left his place, and he was desperate to talk to her. "If she's not going to answer my calls, then I'm going over to her place and talk to her."

Joel had already put the Corvette away in his shop, so he hopped in his everyday car and headed down the road. He hoped Kristi would listen and give him another chance. He was determined to patch things up. As he neared Kristi's place, Joel's palms began to sweat. Could he convince the woman he loved to change her mind about him?

When he pulled in front of Kristi's condo, his stomach clenched. Her car wasn't in the driveway. *I wonder where she could be.*

Joel sat for several minutes, running his hands through his hair. He tried calling her again, but she didn't answer. When her voice mail finally came on, he left a message: "Listen, Kristi, we can't let it end like this. I love you, and we need to talk things through. Please call me."

As his heartbeat continued to race, he decided to drive over to Kristi's parents' house, thinking she might be there. When he turned onto their street, he saw Kristi's car parked in their driveway. At first, he felt relief, but then he realized why she probably was there. *I'll bet Kristi came here to tell her folks about our breakup.*

Joel had always felt a sense of coolness from Kristi's mother, JoAnn, so it wasn't likely she'd have anything positive to say to him right now. He'd gotten along better with her dad, but Paul might side with his daughter and ask Joel to leave.

"Nope, I wouldn't have a chance or a prayer in there," Joel murmured as he drove on by. "I'll give Kristi a few days to calm down, and then I'll call her again."

Chapter 2

When Kristi entered the nursing home Thursday morning, she was greeted with a cheery smile from Dorine Turner, one of the other nurses. "A bouquet of flowers came for you a few minutes ago. I put them in the break room."

Kristi's forehead wrinkled in puzzlement. "Are you sure they're for me?" she asked as she placed her belongings in a cubby. Many of the nursing home residents received flowers, but in all the time Kristi had worked there, no floral delivery had been for her.

Dorine nodded. "I saw your name on the outside of the card."

"Hmm. . . Guess I'll go take a look before I start my rounds."

When Kristi entered the room and spotted the glass vase filled with six lovely pink roses—her favorite flower—she blushed with pleasure. She walked over to the table and cupped the petals gently in her hands, leaning in to smell their delicate scent. *Whoever sent these must know me well. Maybe they're from Mom and Dad.*

When she opened the card attached to the ribbon, she flinched. *To Kristi. Love, Joel.*

Her warm feeling vanished like a candle

flame snuffed out by a gust of air. She bit her lip, then released an irritated huff. *So now Joel thinks he can win me back with flowers?* She shook her head determinedly. *I think not.*

The roses were too pretty to throw out, but there was no way she would take them home. She couldn't believe Joel expected her to take him back and forget everything he'd done to her. *I know what to do. I'll give these flowers to one of the patients.*

After removing the card and tossing it in the trash, Kristi picked up the vase and started down the hall. When she approached Audrey Harrington's room and spotted the elderly woman sitting in a chair by her window, she rapped on the open door.

"Come in." A radiant smile spread across Audrey's wrinkled face when she turned to look at Kristi. "Is it time for my medicine?"

"Not yet." Kristi set the vase on the table beside Audrey's bed. She noticed some gardening magazines stacked neatly next to the lamp. The table looked like it had been cleaned recently with furniture polish, as it glistened in the sunlight shining through the window. Audrey's room was definitely one of the most orderly in the nursing home. While all the rooms received attention from housekeeping, Audrey also made sure her personal items were either lying neatly on the table or tucked away in one of her drawers. "These flowers are for you. I hope you will enjoy them."

"Oh, my!" Audrey's arthritic fingers touched her parted lips. "Who are they from? No one has ever sent me flowers before. At least not since my husband passed away."

"There's a first time for everything." Kristi smiled, placing her hand gently on the elderly woman's slender shoulder. "These pretty roses are from me."

Audrey's hazel-colored eyes blinked rapidly as she gazed at the bouquet, then back at Kristi. "Why, thank you, dear. It was so thoughtful of you."

As much as Kristi disliked Joel trying to worm his way back into her life, she was glad he'd sent the flowers to her place of employment and not her home. It did Kristi's heart good to see the look of joy on Audrey's face as she rose from her chair, shuffled over to the flowers, and bent to smell them.

"The pleasant odor equals their beauty. I hope they last several days."

"I'll make sure when I come in to check on you that the roses get plenty of water," Kristi assured her.

Grinning like a child with a new toy,

Audrey seated herself again, before picking up the worn-looking Bible lying on the foot of her bed. "God answers prayer." She lifted the book and held it to her chest. "I had prayed earlier that something good would happen in my life today, and it has." She gestured to the roses.

Kristi had not even thought to pray such a prayer when she'd gotten up this morning, but if she had, she, too, could proclaim that her prayer had been answered. The "something good" in her life today was seeing the joy she'd brought to a sweet lady who had never had a single visitor in the year she'd been here.

It grieved Kristi to see lonely patients with relatives who either didn't care or lived too far away to come for a visit. Smiling down at Audrey, Kristi decided to take a few minutes each day to visit this sweet lady and any other patients who appeared to be lonely. It would be good for them, as well as her.

Charm, Ohio

When Elsie arrived at her father's place to do more organizing and sorting, she was surprised to find Aunt Verna sitting at the kitchen table, drinking a cup of tea, still dressed in her night clothes.

"*Ach*, you must think I'm a *faulenzer* this morning." A circle of pink erupted on Aunt Verna's cheeks.

"I don't think you're a lazy person at all." Elsie removed her shawl and outer bonnet, hanging them on a wall peg before taking a seat across from her aunt.

"Compared to Lester, I am lazy. He got up early to take care of the horses. Then, as soon as we had our breakfast, he went back out to the barn to do a few more chores." She opened her mouth and yawned loudly. "I slept longer than usual and don't have much get-up-and-go this morning."

"You've probably been working too hard, which is why I'm here to help out."

Aunt Verna tipped her head. "What was it you said?"

Elsie repeated herself.

"Oh, jah, I've been keeping busy."

Elsie stared at the vacant chair positioned at the other end of the table. Tears sprang to her eyes. Oh, how she missed seeing her father in his chair with wheels. It may have seemed quirky to some, but there had always been something fascinating about watching him roll about the room in his special chair. Sometimes he'd even roll into the living room or down the hall to his bedroom. It wasn't that Dad couldn't walk. He simply enjoyed the ride as he pushed himself along with his feet, sometimes singing, whistling, or even playing his harmonica. To Elsie, seeing him do this was a treat.

What a unique character our daed was, she mused. *We never knew what he might say or do.* Growing up with Dad's spontaneity and peculiar habits had kept life interesting, even after Elsie had become an adult.

"Will your sisters be coming to sort through your daed's things today, too?" Aunt Verna's question invaded Elsie's thoughts.

"Uh, no. Doris has a doctor's appointment this morning, and if she feels well enough, she'll work at the restaurant this afternoon." Elsie made sure to speak louder this time.

Aunt Verna's silver-gray brows drew together. "I'm sorry to hear she's still not feeling well. It's good she's finally going to see the doctor."

"I agree."

"What about Arlene? Will she be joining us soon?"

"Not today. Baby Samuel is teething and kind of fussy, so Arlene decided to stay home."

"It's okay. We won't get as much done without their help, but I'm sure the three of us will manage. Although I'm not sure how much Lester will help here in the house. He said during breakfast that there's still plenty of work in the barn to be done."

"We will do the best we can." Elsie left her seat, filled the sink with warm water and detergent, and started washing the dishes.

"You don't have to do that." Aunt Verna got up and put her empty cup in the sink. "These are mine and Lester's breakfast dishes, so I'll take care of them. There are plenty of other things you can do, and you surely didn't come all the way from Millersburg to wash our dirty *gscjaar*."

Elsie knew better than to argue with her aunt. She'd tried it before and hadn't gotten anywhere. Besides, she really did need to get started sorting through more of Dad's things and looking for his will.

"All right then, if you insist." She handed the sponge to her aunt. "Guess I'll head upstairs to the attic and go through some of the items there."

"Good idea. Oh, and don't forget to keep a lookout for your daed's old boots. I still want them, you know."

Elsie nodded, even though she was sure Dad wouldn't have put his boots up there. More than likely he'd tossed them out. Elsie didn't understand Aunt Verna's interest in having Dad's tattered old boots, but if they did turn up, she could certainly have them.

As she made her way upstairs, Elsie thought about how many times she'd climbed these steps when she was a girl. Sometimes, she and her siblings would slide down the stairs on their stomachs, giggling all the way.

Her stomach fluttered at the memory, and she brought her fingers to her lips as a chuckle escaped. *Mama and Dad always told us to stop, otherwise our tummies would get a floor burn, but it was so much fun, we didn't mind. Oh, to be young and carefree again.*

She paused at the door to her old room and peeked inside. Her bed and dresser were no longer there, since her parents had given them to her when she and John got married. Now the bedroom was filled with boxes that hadn't been gone through yet. Elsie thought she would wait on those until one or both of her sisters were here to help. Until it was time to go downstairs and fix lunch, she would concentrate on rummaging through the stuff in the attic.

Turning the knob on the attic door, she decided to leave it open while she worked, so the room could be aired out. Her gaze came to rest on an old wooden chair under a box.

It seemed inviting to sit on while she worked, so she moved the container to the floor and brushed off the chair with a rag she'd brought up with her.

Looking intently around the room for spider webs and seeing none close by, Elsie took a seat and gave the rag a few vigorous shakes to chase off the dust. The chair was kind of wiggly and squeaky. She hoped it wouldn't fall apart while she sat on it. But it was easier on her back than squatting beside every box. Elsie snickered, remembering how this old chair used to be downstairs in the kitchen. It didn't match the others at the table, so when Mama said it wasn't worth keeping, Dad hauled it up to the attic, unwilling to throw it out.

Elsie couldn't believe how much her parents had accumulated over the years. Sometimes sorting things out was like stepping back in time. So many memories... Some happy... Some sad.

"Look what I found!" Elsie announced when she stepped into Joel's old bedroom, where Aunt Verna was on her knees in front of an old trunk.

"What was that?" Still focused on the

open trunk, Aunt Verna tipped her head.

Elsie spoke a little louder. "Look what I found."

Turning to look at her, Aunt Verna let out a whoop. "Ach! You found your daed's old duct-taped boots!" She rose to her feet. "Were they in the *aeddick*?"

"Jah, they were behind a stack of boxes up there." Elsie rubbed the duct tape with her thumb as she set the boots on the floor beside her aunt. "Now when you and Uncle Lester go home, you can take these along."

Aunt Verna grinned. "They'll make such nice planters. I'll probably wait till spring to plant something in them, though. Since fall is here and the temperatures are dipping, there would be no point in putting any kind of *blumme* in these old boots now."

Elsie smiled. "It'll give you something to look forward to in the spring."

"So true. We all need something positive to think about."

"We surely do." Elsie gave her stomach a thump. "I don't know about you, but I'm getting *hungerich*. Should we go downstairs and see if Uncle Lester is ready to eat?"

Aunt Verna nodded and picked up the boots. "You know what, though? I have a feeling he's still outside. If he ever came in, I didn't hear him."

Elsie wasn't sure how to respond. With Aunt Verna's loss of hearing, it was more than possible that Uncle Lester had come into the house without his wife being aware of his presence. And with Elsie having been up on the third floor for the last few hours, she wouldn't have heard her uncle come inside, either.

"Let's go down and see where he is." She placed her hand in the crook of Aunt Verna's arm, and they left the room.

There was no sign of Uncle Lester downstairs, so Elsie headed to the kitchen to start lunch while Aunt Verna went outside to look for him.

She had finished preparing the sandwiches and was about to step outside to call her aunt and uncle, when the back door flew open and Aunt Verna rushed in. "They're gone!" she shouted, frantically waving both hands in the air. "Your daed's mare and her colt are missing!"

Chapter 3

Seeing the look of panic on her aunt's face, Elsie slipped her shoes on, flung the door open, and dashed into the yard.

Uncle Lester stood near the pasture gate, slowly shaking his head. "I thought I closed it when I let 'em into the field this morning, but I either forgot, or it must have blown open." Squinting, he rubbed the back of his neck. "I was in the barn, movin' some bales of hay around, and stepped outside for a breath of fresh air. That's when I discovered the gate was open and the mare and her colt were gone."

"What about my daed's other horses? Did any of them escape?"

"Nope. Just the mare and her foal." He gestured to the pasture. "Can ya see the other horses way out there, grazing?"

Elsie moved closer to the fence. Sure enough, the other horses were where Uncle Lester pointed. She curled her shoulders forward. "Should we walk up the road a ways and see if we can find them, or would it be better to use a buggy?"

"It'll take some time to get a horse and buggy ready, so I'm inclined to walk." He reached under his straw hat and scratched the side of his gray head. "On the other hand, my old arthritic knees won't let me do much walkin' without pain these days. Besides, I have no idea how long the two horses have been missing or how far they've gone from here."

"Why don't you call one of your drivers, Elsie?" Aunt Verna suggested when she joined them by the fence. "If you can get someone to pick Lester up, they can drive up and down the roads looking for those horses."

Elsie tapped her finger against her chin. "That might be a good idea, but it could take a while for me to find someone who's free to come. For now, at least, I think I'll walk down the road a ways and see if I can spot either of the horses." She gestured to her aunt and uncle. "Why don't you two go into the house? I've made some sandwiches. You can eat lunch while I look for the mare and her baby."

Wrinkling her brows, Aunt Verna looked at Uncle Lester. "What'd she say?"

"Said we should go inside and eat lunch while she looks for the *geil*," he shouted.

Aunt Verna shook her head forcibly. "That wouldn't be fair; we should all look for the horses."

Elsie didn't want to hurt her aunt's feelings, but truthfully, she could move much faster if she went looking on her own. She was about to comment, when she spotted Dad's neighbor, Abe Mast, coming up the driveway, leading the mare and her colt.

"I found these critters down by my place," Abe announced. "As soon as I saw 'em, I realized they belonged here."

Elsie breathed a sigh of relief. At least one problem had been solved today. "*Danki* for bringing them back to us."

"That's right," Uncle Lester agreed. "I was worried they might get hit by a car."

"What did you say to that man?" Aunt Verna nudged her husband's arm.

"Said I was worried the horses might get hit by a car!"

"There's no need to shout at me, Lester. I'm not deaf." She straightened her head covering and ambled into the house.

Elsie watched as he followed Aunt Verna, closing the door behind him. Those two sure kept life interesting.

Abe cleared his throat. "I miss your daed, Elsie. There was no one like him. Eustace was not only a good neighbor, but a friend to me as well." He walked up to her with the two horses and passed over their lead ropes.

"Jah. You probably never knew what my daed might say or do sometimes." Holding the ropes, she stood close to the colt and stroked its mane.

"Eustace wasn't afraid to state his opinion on things. He wasn't shy about his faith in the Lord, either." Tears shone in Abe's dark eyes. "Your daed gave me encouragement when I was having doubts about my own beliefs. He saw me through some of the worst of times. Eustace knew the Bible and could quote scriptures so well. He told me to read the Word daily—that it would help get my head thinking straight." A big grin shot across Abe's face. "Need any help getting the horses into the barn?"

"Thanks anyway, but I think I can manage. I'll put them in the corral and bring back your spare tack." Without waiting for Abe's response, Elsie headed for the gate, horses in tow. When she returned with Abe's lead ropes, she asked, "Say, would you like to stay for lunch?"

"It's a nice offer, but I already ate. Besides, I've got work to do at my place."

Elsie smiled. "Thanks again, Abe. Have a nice rest of your day."

After Abe headed for home, Elsie turned toward the house. She was glad the horses were safely home and happy to hear Abe's story about her dad. Hopefully, the rest of the day would be uneventful.

Akron

"I can't believe you're working another double shift," Dorine said when she passed Kristi in the hall. "I'm dead on my feet and more than ready to go home. Figured you would be, too."

Kristi glanced at her watch. It was four o'clock. Normally she'd be getting off work about now. "Working keeps me from thinking too much," she responded. "Besides, I need the extra money right now."

Dorine's gaze flicked upward. "I know what you mean about money. Seems like there's never enough to go around." She gave Kristi's arm a tap. "Just don't spend too much of your time here. Besides burning yourself out, it can get pretty depressing at the nursing home, with so many sick and aging people in our care."

"That doesn't bother me," Kristi replied. "But you're right. If I work too many back-to-back shifts, I will burn out."

"Take the time to do something fun." Dorine moved toward the door. "See you tomorrow, Kristi."

After Kristi waved at her and started down the hall, she decided to check on Audrey. She hadn't seen her in the social room today or even in the patients' lunchroom.

"Are you feeling okay?" Kristi asked when she entered the elderly woman's room and found her sitting in the same chair she had been in that morning.

Audrey turned to look at her and smiled. "I'm fine, but thank you for asking."

"I was worried about you." She moved to stand beside Audrey's chair. "Didn't you eat lunch today?"

"Oh, I ate. Just asked to have my lunch tray brought to my room."

Kristi wondered why Audrey stayed in her room to eat and didn't resist the urge to ask.

"It's not that I didn't want to be with other people," Audrey explained. "I wanted to spend the day in solitude, praying and meditating on God's Word." She lifted the Bible from her lap and nodded at the flowers Kristi had given her. "I've also been enjoying those beauties only God could create."

"Everyone needs to take more time in God's presence and appreciate all the things He's created." Kristi exhaled softly. "Now let me give those roses more water before I forget."

The wrinkles above Audrey's eyes rose as

she tipped her head. "So you're a Christian?"

Kristi nodded, adding more water to the vase. "I'll admit, though, sometimes I get caught up in the busyness of life and neglect my devotions and time of prayer." She dropped her gaze as her throat constricted. "I've been going through a rough time in my life lately, and I haven't sought answers from God." She placed the floral arrangement back on the table beside Audrey's bed.

"Thank you for taking care of my flowers."

"You're most welcome."

Audrey clasped her hands under her chin, in a prayer-like gesture. "If you feel inclined to share your need, I'd be happy to pray for you."

Taking a seat on the edge of Audrey's bed, Kristi shared some of her situation with Joel, without giving all the details. Her throat felt tight and began to ache as she continued to speak. "As much as Joel wants me to take him back, I'm convinced it's not the right thing to do."

Audrey's lips pressed tightly together. "It sounds like your ex-fiancé needs the Lord. Have you been praying for him?"

"Praying for him?" Heat tinged Kristi's face. "Guess I've been too consumed with my anger and disappointment." She sniffed deeply, attempting to thwart oncoming tears.

"I will pray for him, but it's time to move on. Looking back on it all now, I realize we weren't meant to be together."

Joel tried calling Kristi as soon as he finished work that evening. Once again, she didn't answer. "Big surprise," he muttered, directing his truck onto the highway. *Think I'll drop by her house and see if I can catch her there. I'd like to know if she got the flowers I sent.*

The last few days had been hard for Joel, with Kristi not returning his calls, and no word from Elsie about Dad's will. On top of that, he still hadn't landed a job big enough to cover all of his debts.

Disappointed when he pulled up to Kristi's house and saw that her car wasn't there, Joel glanced at his watch. It was five o'clock. *She should've been home from work by now.* He scraped his fingers through his hair, noticing how greasy the roots felt. *Maybe she went to the store. Or she could have gone to the gym to work out.*

Inhaling deeply, Joel made a decision. He'd drop by Kristi's parents' house and see if he could enlist her dad's help. Paul Palmer had always seemed like a reasonable fellow. Whenever he and Kristi got together with her folks in the past, Joel felt as though he and Paul had made a connection. If he could talk to him without JoAnn intervening, he might have a chance.

He turned his truck in the direction of the Palmers' home. When he arrived and saw a dark blue SUV parked in the driveway, he knew at least one of Kristi's parents was there. Hopefully, it was Paul.

Pressing his finger on the doorbell, it only took a few seconds before Paul answered the door.

"Oh, it's you." The man's cool response caused Joel to take a step back. "If you're looking for Kristi, she's not here."

"No, I. . .uh. . .was hoping I could talk to you."

Paul's blue eyes narrowed as he peered at Joel over the top of his reading glasses. "About what?"

"About me and Kristi." Joel moistened his lips with his tongue. "She won't respond to any of my calls, and—"

Paul held up his hand, leaning against the door frame. "Can you blame her, Joel? You've shattered her trust, and she's deeply hurt."

Joel blinked a couple of times to refocus his vision. His eyes felt gritty from lack of sleep. "I realize that, but I need another chance to prove myself." He shifted from one foot to another. "Would you speak to her on my behalf? Tell her how sorry I am and that I'd like to start over?"

Paul's lips pressed together as he shook his head. "I won't play go-between for you. It would be best if you leave Kristi alone and move on with your life so she can do the same."

Scowling, Joel felt an uncomfortable tightness in his chest as he turned away. "Thanks for nothing." He stomped off the porch, gritting his teeth as he made his way back to his vehicle. *There has to be something I can do to get Kristi back. I need to figure out how to make her see she can't live without me.*

Chapter 4

Berlin, Ohio

Doris turned toward the kitchen window, smiling when she saw it was no longer raining. Some puddles remained in the yard, rippling occasionally from the slight wind blowing leaves about. *Guess I'll go to the phone shack to check for messages.*

She glanced at the clock on the far wall. It was six-thirty. Brian would be in from doing his chores soon. There would barely be time for him to eat breakfast before leaving for work, so he wouldn't have a chance to check messages.

Slipping into a heavy sweater, Doris stepped outside, pausing to breathe the chilly air into her lungs. Things always felt so nice after a heavy rain. They'd had three full days of it, and the ground was saturated.

Doris dodged the puddles scattered on the ground as she made her way out to the phone shack. When she opened the door and stepped inside, she saw the light on the answering machine blinking.

Her hands felt like they were clasping icicles when she lowered herself onto the metal chair. Doris flicked the button and listened. The first message was from Elsie, reminding her that she and Arlene planned to be at Dad's place this morning and hoped if Doris wasn't working and felt up to it that she could join them.

I hope I can go. Doris touched her stomach. She'd been faced with some nausea again this morning but had gotten it under control after drinking a cup of ginger tea.

She turned her attention to the next phone message and listened intently, realizing it was her doctor's nurse. "We have the results of your blood tests, Doris. I'm calling to let you know the pregnancy test was positive."

Doris sat in stunned silence with her hand pressed to her chest. "Oh, my."

"Congratulations, Mrs. Schrock. We already have your next appointment scheduled, so please call back to let us know if you're able to come in on that date. We look forward to hearing from you."

This news was almost too good to be true. It was the miracle she and Brian had been praying for.

Without bothering to listen to any of the other messages, Doris left the phone shack and hurried back to the house.

She found Brian in the kitchen, standing

in front of the sink with a glass of water. "Are you all right, Doris? Your cheeks are red as a rose, and you're panting for breath."

"It's cold outside, and I've been to the phone shack." She rushed to his side and clasped his arm. "Oh, Brian, I have the best news."

"What is it? Did one of your sisters find your daed's will?"

"No, this is much better news than anything concerning his will. There was a message for me from Dr. Wilson's nurse."

"What'd she say? Is it a lingering kind of flu you've been dealing with?"

"Jah. I have the baby flu."

Brian blinked a couple of times. "Huh?"

"I said, 'I have the baby flu.'" Doris could hardly contain the laughter bubbling up in her throat.

He tipped his head. "What?"

Tears trickled down her cheeks as she placed both hands on her stomach. "She said my blood tests came back and I am *im e familye weg.*"

Brian's eyes widened. "You. . .you're in a family way?"

"That's correct." Doris rubbed her stomach and smiled. "I can hardly believe it, Brian. God has answered our prayers."

He set the glass on the counter and pulled

her into his arms. "This is the best news. Better than anything I could have imagined."

She leaned her head against his chest as more tears fell. The only thing dampening her joy was the knowledge that her parents would not get to meet their grandchild. But at least Brian's folks were still alive, although Doris wished they lived closer. Geauga County, where her aunt Verna and uncle Lester also lived, was over two hours away.

"I can't wait to share our good news with my sisters," Doris said after she'd dried her eyes. "I'll tell them this morning when I go to Charm to help sort through more of Dad's things."

"Do you think that's a good idea?" Brian gazed into Doris's eyes. "You haven't been feeling well, and now that you're expecting a *boppli*, I don't want you doing too much. In fact, I think you ought to quit your job."

"The nausea is better when I drink ginger tea." She gave his arm a reassuring pat. "I'll be careful not to do too much. As far as my job goes. . . We could use the extra money, so I'd like to keep working awhile longer—at least till I start to show."

"Okay, but if it gets to be too much, you'll need to quit working sooner than that."

"Agreed."

Charm

"Do you think Doris is coming? If so, she ought to be here by now." Arlene looked briefly at the clock above Dad's refrigerator. "It's nine o'clock."

"I called and left her a message last night." Elsie shrugged. "But if she's not feeling well or had to work, she may not be able to come."

Arlene sighed deeply. "Our poor *schwe-schder* has not been feeling up to par for too many days."

"She was supposed to see the doctor last week, but I haven't talked to her since. I'm anxious to find out how the appointment went." Elsie pinched the bridge of her nose. "Guess we should get busy while we're wait-ing to see if Doris shows up. What room do you want to start in today?"

Arlene tapped her toe against the worn linoleum floor. "I'm not sure. Do you have a preference?"

"Not really. I worked in the attic when I was here last week, but we still have a lot more boxes up there to go through."

"I can only imagine. It seems boxes are in nearly every room of this house, not to mention the barn and buggy shed. Sure will be glad once we get through all of it."

"Too bad Uncle Lester and Aunt Verna went home last Saturday. We could still use some extra help."

Arlene glanced at baby Samuel, lying in his playpen. "If my little guy wakes up and starts fussing, I won't be much help for a while, either."

"We could ask some of the women in our church district to help, but Dad's things are personal, and only we know what we want to keep or throw out."

"True." Arlene moved toward the stove. "The water's hot now. Would you like a cup of tea?"

"That'd be nice. I'll get out the cups and put our teabags in." Elsie placed the cups on the table.

Arlene waited for her sister to add the tea bags before she poured the hot water. Opening the refrigerator to get some cream, her gaze came to rest on the pie Elsie had brought. Her mouth watered, thinking how good it would taste. It was tempting to sample a piece now, but it would be better to wait until later to cut the pie.

"How are things working out with your son staying here since Aunt Verna and Uncle Lester left?" Arlene asked Elsie.

"From what Glen said when I got here this morning, everything's been fine. He's been getting up early to take care of the horses and does some other chores after he gets home from work."

"I bet it's kind of lonely for him being here all alone."

"If it is, he hasn't complained. He's probably glad to be by himself, after spending a good piece of the day at work with his daed and the other fellows John has working for him." Elsie laughed. "I think Blaine misses his big brother, though he'd never admit it."

"That's often how it is with siblings. Sometimes Doug and Scott don't always get along, but when Doug's old enough to move out of the house, I'm sure Scott will miss him."

"You're probably right."

They'd just started drinking their tea when Arlene heard the whinny of a horse from outside. "I'll bet that's Doris."

"Oh, good. It must mean she's feeling better." Elsie jumped up. "Think I'll go help her unhitch the horse and get it put in the corral."

Arlene smiled. "I'll make sure to have a cup of tea ready for Doris when you come in."

"I'm sure she'll appreciate it on this brisk fall morning." Elsie wrapped her shawl around her shoulders and slipped out the back door.

While Arlene waited for her sisters to come in, she fixed another cup of tea. Glancing at the wall peg near the back door, she noticed her father's old hat. He had duct-taped part of the brim, like he'd done with his worn-out boots.

Sniffing, she reached for a tissue to dry her eyes and wipe her nose. The old hat was reminiscent of Dad, but she doubted anyone would want it. And they sure couldn't take it to the thrift store. Nobody would buy a hat in that condition, even if the price was reasonable.

As Arlene continued to gaze at the hat, a memory from her childhood came to mind. When Joel was five years old, he'd found Dad's straw hat somewhere in the barn. He had emerged from the building wearing the hat, which was much too big for him and nearly covered his eyes. Then he'd sauntered over to the swing, where Arlene was pushing Doris, and announced, "Someday, when I'm big like *Daadi*, I'm gonna be rich. Then I can buy whatever I want."

Arlene shuddered, gripping the back of Dad's chair. Little did she realize back then that her brother's quest for money would continue into his adult life. All Joel seemed to care about was finding the will so he could get his share of the money.

We all could use money, Arlene thought. *But I'd rather have Dad here than any fortune he may have left us. Nothing on earth is more important than my family.*

The back door opened, and Doris and Elsie stepped in, putting an end to Arlene's musings. "I'm glad you could make it." She gave Doris a hug. "How are you feeling this morning?"

"I was a little nauseous when I first woke up, but a cup of ginger tea took care of it." Doris lifted the plastic sack she held. "I brought more teabags with me, in case I feel sick to my stomach again."

"I heard you went to the doctor's last week. Did you find out what was wrong with you?" Arlene questioned.

"They took blood tests, and I got the results this morning." Doris's face broke into a wide smile. "I'm im e familye weg."

"Ach, my!" Elsie, who stood closest to Doris, gave her a hug. "That's such good news."

"Congratulations!" Arlene rushed forward and wrapped her arms around both of her sisters. She quoted Psalm 107:1: "O give thanks unto the Lord, for he is good: for his mercy endureth for ever."

For the next half hour, the sisters sat at the table, drinking tea and rejoicing over Doris's good news.

"As nice as this is, I think we ought to get busy and do some sorting now." Doris pushed away from the table.

"You're right," Elsie agreed. "Should we all work in the same room, or would you rather each take a separate room?"

"It might be better if we work separately," Arlene replied. "If we work together, we'll be apt to visit and get less sorting done."

"Maybe I'll continue working in the attic." Elsie smiled at Doris. "Would you mind going through some boxes in your old room, and Arlene can sort boxes in the room she used to sleep in? That way, we'll all be upstairs, and if any of us needs something, we'll be able to hear each other."

Doris nodded, and Arlene did the same. "If you start feeling sick to your stomach or get tired and want to lie down, please don't hesitate to do so." Arlene touched Doris's arm. "There's no way we can get all the sorting done today, so we shouldn't push ourselves too hard."

"I'll rest if I need to."

"Did either of you find Dad's will?" Elsie asked when the sisters stopped working to fix lunch.

"The only thing I found were a lot of old copies of *The Budget*, plus way too many catalogs." Doris groaned. "I don't understand why Dad thought he had to keep all those."

"I don't either," Arlene agreed. "All I can say is Mama was lenient on Dad's behalf. Each time one of us moved out, she'd let him put his things in the empty rooms. Using our old bedrooms to store boxes only gave him more places to keep all that junk."

"To Dad, it wasn't junk. He must have had a purpose for all his collections." Elsie picked up the box of pens she'd found in the attic.

"Maybe we shouldn't throw out any of the magazines or catalogs until we've had a chance to look through every page." Arlene took out a loaf of bread to make sandwiches.

"Why would we want to do that?" Doris questioned.

"It may seem strange, but Dad could have stuck his will inside one of the magazines or even at the bottom of one of the boxes."

Doris went to the refrigerator to get the mustard, mayonnaise, meat, and cheese. "If we take time to thumb through every magazine, catalog, and newspaper, I'll be helping here sorting till my boppli's born—maybe longer."

Elsie was about to comment when she heard a familiar rumble. She went to the window and watched as a tractor entered the yard. "Henry Raber is here, and it looks like he brought his hund."

Arlene gestured to the food Doris placed on the counter. "There's plenty to make several sandwiches. We should invite him to stay for lunch."

"I'll bet he came over because he misses Dad so much," Doris interjected. "Poor Henry has no family living in the area. I'm sure he gets lonely."

"He and Dad were best friends, even though Henry was New Order and Dad was Old Order. Their friendship was special." Elsie opened the back door just as Henry, holding Peaches under one arm and a book in his other hand, stepped onto the porch.

"I won't trouble you." Henry handed Elsie the book. "I borrowed this from your daed some time ago and thought I'd better return it. I heard your son Glen was staying here and hoped I might find him at home."

"Glen's at work," Elsie explained. "I'm here today with Doris and Arlene. We've been going through some of Dad's things." She glanced at the book—a fiction novel set in the Old West. "Why don't you keep this, Henry? I'm sure Dad would want you to have it."

Henry nodded slowly, his eyes misting as Elsie handed the book to him. "I have many good memories about Eustace. It's hard to believe he's gone."

"It is for us as well." She opened the door wider. "We're about to have lunch. Why don't you come in and join us?"

"Oh, I don't want to put you out." Henry turned his head in the dog's direction. "Besides, I have Peaches with me, and if I put her back in the cage, she'll whine and carry on like a squalling baby."

"It's okay, bring her in. She can lie on the throw rug near the door." Elsie felt sure the dog would stay there because she'd witnessed how well-behaved Peaches was before.

After Henry came inside and washed his hands, he told Peaches to lie on the rug. Everyone gathered around the table, and once their silent prayer was said, Elsie circled the table and passed around the platter of sandwiches. As they ate, their conversation covered several topics, including the weather.

"Can't say I'm lookin' forward to snow, but I'm sure it'll be comin'." Henry's bushy eyebrows drew together. "I'm thinkin' about spending the winter in Florida, like so many other Amish and Mennonite folks my age do."

"Maybe you should." Doris handed Henry the bag of chips she'd brought along to share. "I bet Peaches would love romping on the beach."

"Jah." He looked over at Peaches. "I was hoping Eustace would want to go there with me, but I guess going with my hund would be better than not goin' at all." He motioned to Dad's old hat on the wall peg. "I'll never forget the day I came to visit your daed and he was wearing that old hat held together with duct tape. Seeing it hangin' there now makes me feel as though he might come through the door any time. Course," he quickly added, "I know it's not gonna happen."

In a spontaneous decision, Elsie rose from her chair and took the hat down. "How would you like to have this, Henry?" She held it out to him.

"Ach, no, I can't take that. You already gave me the book. Besides. . ." He lowered his gaze. "It's your daed's special hat."

"It's okay, Henry. I want you to have it. We have plenty of other things here to remember him by." She smiled. "Besides, none of us have a reason to wear a straw hat. As long as you're wearing it, it'll be put to good use."

His eyes filled with tears as he took the hat from her. "Danki. Think I'll hang it in my kitchen. Then every time I look at it, I'll think of your daed."

Seeing how choked up Henry had become, Elsie moved over to the refrigerator and took out the pie she'd brought for dessert. "Who wants a piece of millionaire pie?" she asked.

Doris and Arlene held up their hands, but Henry continued to sit, while staring at the hat.

"Henry, would you like piece of millionaire pie?" Arlene asked.

He looked over at her and blinked. "I've never heard of millionaire pie. Did one of you make up the name on account of your daed?"

Elsie shook her head. "No, it really is the name of the pie." She placed it on the table while Doris got out four plates and forks. She was thankful Henry had stopped by today. Having him here made her feel somehow closer to Dad.

"So what do you hear from your bruder these days?" Henry asked.

A thin line of wrinkles formed above Doris's brows. "We haven't seen Joel since Dad's funeral."

Henry pushed a strand of gray hair aside and scratched behind his ear. "That's too bad.

You'd think he'd want to spend time with his sisters."

Elsie clutched the folds in her dress. She wasn't about to tell Henry what she thought of her selfish brother, but she couldn't help wondering why she hadn't heard from Joel in several days. *Has he been too busy to call me, or has my brother decided to be patient and wait for me to let him know once we find the will?*

Chapter 5

Berlin

It was the last Saturday of October, and for the first time since her breakup with Joel, Kristi felt a sense of excitement. Moments ago, she and Mom had left the quilt shop where they'd taken their first quilting lesson. Since her Saturdays were free now and she needed something fun to do, learning how to quilt seemed like a good idea. It was also an opportunity for her and Mom to spend time together, doing something they both enjoyed. Kristi had certainly enjoyed today's lesson, although most of the morning had been spent learning the basics of quilting and cutting the pieces of material they would use to make their quilts. Kristi had chosen two shades of purple for the queen-size quilt she planned to put on her bed.

Another reason she liked the class was because their Amish instructor was kind and patient. Kristi's desire to know more about the Amish way of life could be somewhat fulfilled by spending time with Mattie Troyer. It was a shame she'd have no connection with Joel's sisters now that she and Joel had no plans to be married.

"You're awfully quiet over there." Mom removed one hand from the steering wheel and tapped Kristi's arm. "It was beginning to feel like I was alone in the car."

Kristi's lips parted slightly. "Sorry, Mom. I've been deep in thought."

"Mind if I ask what you were thinking about?"

"Oh, nothing exciting—just reflecting on our first quilting class. I enjoyed it so much and appreciated how patient our teacher was with all my questions."

"Yes, she was very kind and helpful. I had fun, too, and look forward to our class next week."

"Same here." Kristi pulled down the visor to check her hair.

"Are you sure you don't mind taking a side trip to Charm so I can get more of that good cheese I bought for your dad the last time we were here?"

"I don't mind at all. I'll probably buy some cheese, too." Looking in the visor mirror, Kristi pulled her hairband off and brushed every strand back in place before securing it in a ponytail.

As they drew closer to Charm, she spotted the road she and Joel took to his dad's place. She was on the verge of asking Mom to turn there so she could see it but changed her mind. One of Joel's sisters, or even Joel, might be there, and it could be awkward. It was best to say nothing and keep going. If she even pointed out the road and said it led to Eustace Byler's home, Mom might say she was better off without Joel. Kristi didn't need the reminder; she still felt she had done the right thing. She would continue to pray for Joel, as Audrey had suggested, but it wouldn't be for them to get back together. She'd ask God to help Joel see the importance of developing a close relationship with his sisters and their families and, most of all, to know God personally.

"Say, I have an idea." Mom broke into Kristi's thoughts a second time. "When we leave the cheese store in Charm, why don't we head up to Walnut Creek and eat lunch at Der Dutchman? I really enjoyed our meal the last time we went there."

"That's fine with me." Kristi leaned back in her seat. Being in Amish country made her feel nostalgic. *If only things had worked for me and Joel.*

Walnut Creek, Ohio

Doris was glad her shift would end at two o'clock. She'd arrived at the restaurant early today to serve the breakfast crowd, but a lot more people had come in for lunch. In addition to a few waves of nausea she'd experienced during her shift, her feet hurt from being on them so long. Fortunately, she only had another hour to go; then she'd head for home and take a nap.

Maybe Brian was right when he said I should quit my job. But with a baby coming, we need the extra money, so I'll try to keep working as long as I can.

Glancing toward her section of tables, Doris noticed the hostess seating two women. One she recognized immediately—Joel's girlfriend. She moved over to their table. "It's nice to see you again, Kristi."

Blinking rapidly, Kristi offered Doris a brief smile. "Oh, hi. I'd forgotten you worked here." She motioned to the auburn-haired woman sitting across from her. "This is my mother, JoAnn. Mom, I'd like you to meet Joel's sister Doris."

"It's nice to meet you." Doris lifted the pencil and order pad from her apron pocket.

"Actually, this isn't our first meeting." JoAnn glanced briefly out the window, then back at Doris. "My daughter and I ate lunch here a few months ago. You were our waitress then, as well. But that was before Kristi had been formally introduced to you the day of your father's funeral." She paused and moistened her lips. "I'm so sorry for your loss."

Doris fought for control. Nearly every time someone offered their condolences, she teared up. "Thank you," she murmured.

"How's your family?" Kristi asked. "Are you and your sisters getting along okay?"

"Under the circumstances, we're doing the best we can." She paused. "How's Joel? None of us have seen him since the funeral."

Kristi's cheeks flushed as she spun the bracelet around her wrist. "Umm. . .Joel and I aren't together anymore."

Doris drew in a quick breath, nearly dropping her order pad. "I—I'm so sorry. I didn't know."

"It's all right. If you want to hear what happened, feel free to give me a call some evening, and I'll explain everything." Kristi picked up the menu in front of her.

"Oh, okay." Doris had almost forgotten she and Kristi had exchanged phone numbers the day of Dad's funeral. She was curious to know why Kristi and Joel had broken up, so she would definitely give her a call. Based on Joel's past history with Anna, Doris felt sure the breakup was his fault.

Akron

When Joel stopped working at two o'clock to eat lunch, he decided to check his cell phone for messages. He'd been busy remodeling a closet for a newly married couple and had absentmindedly left his phone in the truck. Due to the stress from his breakup with Kristi and her refusal to return any of his calls, he'd forgotten a lot of things lately. Joel was consumed by his desire to be with Kristi. He couldn't believe she wouldn't talk to him or respond to any of his text messages.

Maybe I should send her more flowers. Joel climbed into his truck and picked up his cell phone. *Doesn't she realize how desperate I am to get her back?*

Joel typed in his password, hoping one of the messages he'd received was from Kristi. The first two were prospective customers. The next one was the carpenter to whom he still owed money. The final message was from Elsie, asking Joel to check with Kristi to see if they could come to supper one evening.

"There's no point replying to that message," he mumbled, placing the cell phone on the passenger's seat. "Sorry, Sis, but you're a little too late. And what about Dad's will? You made no mention of that."

Joel's face tightened as he rubbed at the knots in the back of his neck. Elsie promised to get back to him about Dad's will, but so far there had been no word. Did it mean they hadn't found it yet, or was she keeping it from him? "Could Dad have cut me out of his will?" Joel grunted. "He'd better not have done something like that."

He sucked in a couple of deep breaths, trying to calm himself. Elsie had always been a straightforward person. If they'd found the will, she would have said so. He reached over to the passenger seat and grabbed his lunch pail. Looking inside, he decided to start with the bag of chips. While he ate them, he thought about how to deal with his situation. He still had another hour or two before he finished working today.

Clutching the steering wheel, Joel decided he would go home, take a shower, get a bite to eat, and head to Charm. He was going to take the quest for Dad's will into his own hands. Surely it couldn't be that hard to find.

Charm

When Joel arrived at his father's house, he wasn't surprised to see all the windows completely dark. He figured by now his aunt and uncle would have returned to their home. Since no one lived here anymore, it was his perfect opportunity to look around.

He pulled his truck up near the barn and

turned off the engine. Fortunately, he'd had the good sense to bring a flashlight along, because it would have been nearly impossible to find his way to the front door in the dark.

Stepping onto the porch, Joel turned the knob and was surprised to find the door locked. He kicked it and gritted his teeth. In all the years he'd grown up in this house, Dad had never locked any of the doors. Joel figured his sisters had locked the place to keep anyone from breaking in.

Guess in a way, that's what I'm doing, he thought as he headed around back, hoping to find that door unlocked. Irritation welled when he discovered it, too, was locked.

"Sure wish I had a key," Joel mumbled. "Now I've gotta check every window and hope one is open."

He shined the light on the first window. In so doing, he caught sight of the basement door. *Maybe that's unlocked.*

Making his way carefully down the stairs, he turned the knob. *Bingo!* The door opened. Joel figured there had to be a gas or kerosene lamp down there somewhere, so he shined his flashlight around until he found one. After lighting it, he began his search—looking through box after box for anything that resembled a will.

This could take forever. He blew out his breath. *If I don't find something soon, I may as well head home and come back another day when I'm not working and have plenty of time to look around.*

Joel had to be desperate to be in Dad's basement, searching through all this junk. "Really, what are the odds the will would be down here anyway?" he muttered.

He decided to check another box, but just as he opened the lid, the kerosene lamp went out. *Oh, great.*

Feeling his way, Joel moved slowly across the room, hoping he was heading in the direction of the door. After he'd turned on the lamp, he'd stupidly laid his flashlight down, and now that he was in the dark, he couldn't find it. If he could make it to the door, he'd have to find his car in the blackness of night.

Joel continued to move around and managed to knock something over. The metallic sound resonated throughout the basement, and he reached out to see if he could tell what it was. From the feel of the object, he was fairly certain it was one of the old milk cans Dad was so fond of. Grunting, Joel moved it aside. Trying to walk through the maze of clutter wasn't working out too well, so he went down on his knees. As he crawled across the floor, he moved his hand around, searching for the flashlight. A chill went up Joel's spine when he heard a noise behind him. *What was that?*

Suddenly, an intense light shone in his face, stinging his eyes. A deep voice shouted, "What are you doing here?"

Chapter 6

"Maybe I should be the one asking 'What are you doing here?'" Joel blurted, when he realized the young man holding the flashlight in front of his face was Elsie's son Glen.

"I've been stayin' here since Aunt Verna and Uncle Lester went home."

"Oh, I see." Joel found his own flashlight and clambered to his feet. "How come the house is so dark? It was only seven o'clock when I got here. I doubt you were in bed."

"Just got back from havin' supper at my folks. Sure was surprised to see your truck parked out by the barn." Glen pointed his flashlight at Joel again but avoided his face. "What were you doin' down here in the dark, and how'd ya get in?"

"The basement door was unlocked, and not that it's any of your business, but I've been looking for my dad's will."

"My mamm and her sisters have been doin' that. Do they know you're here?"

"No, they don't, but even if they did, I don't care." Joel tightened his fingers around the flashlight. "This is my dad's house, and I have as much right to be here as anyone else in the family."

"So, did ya find Grandpa's will?" Glen leaned against a stack of folding chairs.

"Not yet, but I'll do more looking tomorrow."

Glen's eyebrows squished together. "You're comin' back on Sunday?"

"I won't have to come back, because I'm already here." Joel didn't know why he hadn't thought of it before, but since he was at his dad's house and didn't have to work tomorrow, he may as well spend the night. It didn't matter that tomorrow was Sunday, because he had no plans to go to church. In fact, he hadn't attended even once since Kristi broke up with him. What would be the point? He'd only be going to impress her, which probably wouldn't work, since she'd no doubt be there with her folks. Since Kristi's dad didn't want Joel bothering his daughter, Joel figured he'd better stay clear of Kristi's parents.

"What are you saying—that you plan to spend the night here?" Glen stared at Joel as though in disbelief.

"Yeah, that's right. I'll bed down in my old room tonight."

"There are a lot of boxes up there. You'd probably have to move some of 'em to get to the bed."

"It won't bother me. I'll do what needs to be done in order to make the room comfortable. Maybe I'll look through those boxes before I go to bed." Joel pointed toward the stairs that led up to the kitchen. "Let's head on up."

Glen led the way, as he continued to speak. "You can do whatever you want, but it won't do ya no good. I think the boxes in your old room have already been gone through, and no will was found."

Joel's pulse quickened. This twenty-year-old man seemed determined to keep him from spending the night. But Joel wasn't about to be dissuaded. If he didn't find what he was looking for tonight, he'd continue his search in the morning.

The following morning, Joel woke up to the sound of soft winds blowing against his bedroom window. He groaned, slowly pulling the covers over his head. It felt like a herd of horses had trampled his back. The mattress on his old bed was a lot harder than he remembered.

He let out a few breaths, while slowly rising from the bed, then winced when his bare feet touched the cold hardwood floor. He might as well have been standing on a frozen lake. Joel's trailer house had carpeting in the bedroom, so he wasn't used to walking on a frigid floor as soon as he stepped out of bed. Stretching his arms overhead, Joel ambled over to the window and looked out. The sun was hidden behind the clouds, but at least it wasn't raining.

He hurried to get dressed, and shortly after, caught a whiff of coffee brewing. *I could sure use some caffeine to kick-start my day.*

Closing the door to his room, Joel hurried down the stairs, following the enticing scent. He found his nephew in the kitchen, slathering peanut butter on a piece of toast.

"Mornin'. Coffee's ready if ya want some, and there's bread to make toast. Or if you'd rather have cold cereal, there's some of that, too." Glen pointed across the room.

"I'm good with coffee for now." Joel took a mug out of the cupboard and filled it with the steaming brew. "Thanks for making the coffee." He took a sip and smacked his lips. "This hits the spot. Not too bad at all."

"You really oughta eat some breakfast. My mamm always says, 'Everyone needs a hearty breakfast to begin the day.'"

"Your mom's not here, so I'll do as I please." Joel pulled a chair toward him and took a seat at the table, ignoring his nephew's finger tapping on the tabletop. *Glen probably wishes I wasn't invading his space. Well, if he does, it's too bad. I'm here, and I plan to make the day count for something, even if I don't locate the will. If I look long enough, at least I'll know where it isn't.*

"How long will you be sticking around?" Glen's serous brown eyes seemed to bore right into Joel's soul.

He shrugged his shoulders. "Don't know yet. Could be a good part of the day."

"You gonna keep lookin' for Grandpa's will?" Glen got up to warm his coffee.

"It's important for somebody to find it... and soon."

"Sure seems odd no one's located it yet. Makes me wonder if there even is a will. What do you think, Joel?" Glen bit into his toast and brushed the fallen crumbs off his black vest.

Joel's internal temperature heated as he gripped his fingers around the handle of his mug. "There has to be a will. My daed was no *dummkopp*. I'm sure he'd want to provide for his kinner." He scratched his cheek, unsure of why he'd spoken several Amish words. When Joel walked away from his heritage, it took a while to quit speaking Pennsylvania Dutch, but he'd left it behind. Except for the few words he'd shared with Kristi, Joel hadn't spoken it in a long time. *Being here in Dad's house and speaking to Glen must be what caused me to revert.*

"Come to think of it, my mamm said Aunt Verna told her that Grandpa did make out a will." Glen finished eating his toast and washed it down with a swig of coffee. "The only trouble is Aunt Verna can't remember where he put it."

"That's ridiculous. He should have told someone else where it is." Joel wondered if his dad had gone to a lawyer to have the will made up, or if he'd done his own and had it notarized. He guessed the latter, because if Dad had a lawyer, surely one of Joel's sisters or Aunt Verna would know who it was and have contacted him by now. *Don't know why Dad had to be so closemouthed about things.*

"Whelp, I need to get outside and hitch my *gaul* to the buggy." Glen pushed away from the table and put his dishes in the sink, rinsing them off. Then he brushed off his dark-colored dress trousers, where a few crumbs had stuck. "Today's a church Sunday for our district, and I don't want to be late." He turned to face Joel. "Would ya like to go with me? My folks, as well as my brother and sisters, will be there. I'm sure they'd like to see you."

"Yeah, I figured by the way you're dressed

that it was a church day. I won't be going with you, but I will walk out to the barn. It'll be nice to see my dad's horses." Joel grabbed his jacket and followed Glen out the door.

After they entered the barn, Joel watched Glen get his horse ready and lead it outside to the buggy. "Do you ever take my dad's buggy horse out for a ride?" he asked.

Glen shook his head. "No way! That crazy gaul is too spirited for me."

"He will only get worse if he isn't taken out sometimes." Joel slid his hand into his jacket pocket and pulled out a piece of gum. A memory from the past popped into his head. Dad used to carry gum in his pockets. Whenever Joel went out to the barn to help clean or take care of the horses, he was usually rewarded with a stick of gum. Of course, he was just a boy then, and any little treat from Dad was appreciated.

Glen broke into Joel's musings. "You're most likely right about Grandpa's horse, but my daed said he'd take care of doing that."

"Bet I could make the horse do what I wanted." With legs spread wide, Joel thrust out his chest. "I grew up with Dad's horses. I could always make them do what I wanted."

Glen tipped his head slightly but made no comment.

"Has anyone in the family talked about selling Dad's horses? It makes no sense to keep them, now that Dad is gone." Joel pulled his fingers through the sides of his hair. "Besides, the money could be split among me and my sisters."

"That's something you'd have to discuss with them." Glen led his horse to the front of the buggy shafts.

"Yeah, I'll do that." Joel caught sight of Glen's straw hat lying on the floor of his open buggy. He wouldn't be wearing it today, however. For church, all Amish men wore their black dress hats. He reached in and picked up the hat. Holding it brought back memories from when he was Amish. It was strange how moments like this made him feel a sense of nostalgia and actually helped him relax. Other times, certain thoughts from his past put him on edge or seemed like nothing more than a distant dream.

Farmerstown

"Say, Mom, can me and Scott go over to Grandpa's after church today so we can jump on the trampoline?" Arlene's son Doug asked as they finished eating breakfast.

Arlene pursed her lips. "I don't think so,

Son. It's not a good idea for you boys to be hanging around over there alone."

"I wanna go, too," Lillian spoke up.

Her sister, Martha, bobbed her head in agreement. "If we all go, then none of us will be alone."

"Our daughter has a point," Arlene's husband interjected. "Besides, now that Glen is staying at your daed's house, they'll have adult supervision."

Arlene frowned. "Glen is not a self-sufficient adult yet. He's twenty years old, and until he moved into Dad's place, which is only temporary, he lived at home."

"He's old enough to stay by himself. And he has a full-time job, so I think he's capable of supervising our kinner today, don't you?"

Arlene sighed. "I suppose you're right." She looked at Doug. "Just make sure you and your siblings are *achtsam* today. No craziness on the trampoline, okay?"

"We'll be careful," the boy promised.

"Are you going to ride your bikes, or would you like me to take you there with my horse and buggy?" Larry questioned.

"We'll ride our bikes." Doug looked at his siblings. "Is that okay with you?"

Scott, Lillian, and Martha nodded.

Smiling at Arlene, Larry reached over and

patted her arm. "While the kinner are at your daed's place, you should take a nap. You've been working too hard lately, trying to keep up with all your chores here, plus helping your sisters sort through your daed's things. If you're not careful, you're gonna wear yourself down and may even get *grank*."

"I won't get sick from doing a little work, so please don't worry." She rose from her seat and scooped her dishes into the sink. "Hurry now, everyone. We don't want to be late for church."

Charm

After searching for the will for two hours, Joel decided he needed some fresh air. *Think I'll take Dad's closed-in buggy and hitch up his spirited horse. I'll bet he's not nearly as hard to handle as Glen thinks.*

Thirty minutes later, Joel plunked Glen's straw hat on his head, climbed into the buggy in an easygoing manner, and took up the reins. It felt strange to be sitting on the right-hand side of the buggy, in readiness to take the horse out on the road. Joel had become used to driving his cars and truck, where he felt more in control. He'd never admit it to his nephew, but Joel felt a bit vulnerable right now.

Don't be such a coward, he chided himself. *If you learn how to ride a bike, you never forget what to do. Same goes for driving a horse and buggy.*

With a renewed sense of confidence, Joel directed the horse up the driveway and onto the road. So far, the animal was behaving, and he began to relax. The sound of the horse's hooves hitting the pavement caused Joel's breaths to slow down. He pictured himself when he was younger, riding in the buggy with his family on their way to church every other Sunday. He would watch his father intently as he guided the horse down the road. There was something about controlling a thousand-pound steed that Joel had found intriguing, and he'd wanted nothing more than to try it himself. He had been given a pony when he was a boy, but training the small animal to pull the pony-cart had been too easy.

Joel reflected on the first time Dad had let him drive the horse and buggy. He'd been eleven years old and had begged to try it. His lips curved into a smile. *Dad thought I was too young, but I proved him wrong when he finally handed me the reins.*

A mile or so up the road, something spooked the horse, which caused Joel's thoughts to scatter. The spirited gelding began to act up, flipping his head from side to side, while balking at Joel's every request. Then, as if he'd been stung by a bee, the critter took off like a flash. "Whoa, boy!" he hollered, pulling back on the reins. "There's no need to rush."

Joel heaved a sigh of relief when he finally got the animal under control and going at a slower, even pace. "What's wrong with you?" He spoke to the horse with assurance. "Are you trying to make me look bad?"

Joel was surprised when the gelding responded with a whinny. *Maybe he was purposely testing me, and now he knows who's boss.*

Rounding the next bend, he spotted an open buggy heading in the opposite direction. He recognized the driver immediately—Anna Detweiler. She didn't wave while passing, so Joel figured Anna hadn't recognized him. Of course, being in the closed buggy, he wouldn't have been as easy to recognize as if he'd been driving an open rig.

Joel's thoughts took him back to the months he'd courted Anna and all the fun things they'd done together. He remembered how they used to play volleyball with some of their friends in the evenings during the summer. The soles of Joel's feet would tickle as he maneuvered on the grass, trying to win a point for his team. Joel wasn't as good at the game as Anna; she was a natural. She'd tried to show him the correct way to serve the ball, by tossing it in the air, striking it with a hand or lower part of her arm. But Joel continued to mess up when it was his turn to serve.

He couldn't help but smile when he thought about her. In addition to being pretty, and a good volleyball player, Anna was easygoing, smart, and had a special connection with children, which was what probably made her want to be a teacher. Joel, on the other hand, had never been patient with children. They usually got on his nerves. Of course, if they were his own kids, he might feel differently.

His brows pulled in as he pinched the bridge of his nose. *What would my life be like now if I'd stayed Amish?* He clutched the reins tighter as he weighed the issue. *Did I make a mistake breaking up with Anna to go English? If we'd gotten married, could I have learned to be content living the Plain life?*

Chapter 7

Joel guided the horse and buggy into his dad's yard and was surprised to see five children playing near the house. As he drew closer, he realized four of them were Arlene's—Doug, Scott, Martha, and Lillian. Joel didn't recognize the other boy. He figured it was one of their friends from school or church district.

He climbed down from the buggy and secured the horse. Holding Glen's straw hat in his hand, Joel stood a few minutes, watching the children play. Fortunately, they were preoccupied and hadn't seen him yet. "Great! The last thing I need is five rambunctious kids hanging around, asking a bunch of questions and distracting me from looking for Dad's will," Joel mumbled under his breath. *I'll have to make sure they stay outside or convince them to go home.*

Joel had begun unhitching the horse when Scott ran up to him. "Hey, Uncle Joel! I didn't know you were gonna be here today." His face glowed pink—most likely from playing.

"I didn't expect you, either." He squinted at the boy. "What are doing here, anyway?"

Scott grinned up at him. "Me, my brother and sisters, and my friend Alvin came to jump on the trampoline Grandpa bought a few years ago."

"Do your folks know you're here?"

"Jah. My daed and mamm said it was fine 'cause our cousin Glen's stayin' here at the house." Scott tipped his head back and stared up at Joel with a curious expression. "Why did you come, and why were you drivin' Grandpa's horse and buggy?"

Already with the questions. "I came to look through some of my daed's things, and I needed some fresh air, so I took the gaul and buggy out for a ride." Joel's jaw tightened. He'd spoken some Pennsylvania-Dutch again.

Scott's eyes blinked rapidly. "Did ya have trouble with the gaul? Grandpa used to say his gaul could be a feisty one."

"At first he tried to act up, but I got him under control." Joel led the horse to the barn and grimaced when he noticed Scott trailing behind him. He wished the kid would go back and play.

Scott followed Joel into the horse's stall. "Did ya bring your harmonica with ya today?"

"No."

The boy's shoulders drooped. "Sure wish ya had."

"I don't take my harmonica everywhere I go."

"I was hopin' you could teach me how to play it. If ya had the mouth harp with ya right now, then—"

"Maybe some other time." Joel focused his gaze on the horse's mane and began brushing it. He was about to suggest that Scott go back to jumping on the trampoline, when Doug darted into the barn. Joel's neck stiffened as he lowered his arm. *Terrific! Now I have two of them to deal with.*

"Sure am surprised to see you here." Doug crossed his arms and stared up at Joel. "Did my folks know you were comin'?"

Joel's knuckles whitened as he continued to brush the horse. "No, and I didn't see a need to tell them." He managed to keep his composure, but his patience was wearing thin.

Doug looked at Scott and his eyebrows lifted slightly, but neither of them commented.

When Joel finished with the horse, he hurried from the barn. The boys were right on his heels.

Joel stopped when he got to the house, then turned to face them. "If you kids and your friend want to jump on the trampoline, that's fine with me, but I've got things I need to do in the house. So unless you have to use the bathroom or get a drink, would you please stay outside? I don't want to be disturbed."

They nodded soberly.

"By the way, where's Glen? I didn't see his horse in the barn."

"Guess he ain't home from church yet," Doug answered. "He has farther to go than we do. Besides, he may have gone to his folks' house after church. Or maybe he went to visit his *aldi*."

"Didn't know he had a girlfriend."

"A lot of stuff goes on here that you don't know." Doug's tone was so matter of fact, it took Joel by surprise.

He frowned. "I'm sure there is."

Scott tapped Joel's arm. "Ya know, Uncle Joel, if ya smiled once in a while, people might like you better."

Taken aback, Joel forced a hard smile. "Maybe you're right, but I don't have much to smile about these days."

"There's always something to smile about. Our daed says laughter's good medicine." Doug rocked back slightly on his heels as he looked up at Joel. "In case ya didn't know, that's right outa the Bible."

Joel rolled his eyes as he bit the inside of his cheek. If he hung around here much longer, one or both of the boys would probably follow him inside and start preaching or quoting more scriptures at him. He glanced at his truck, still parked by the barn. Since Glen hadn't returned from church yet, Joel thought he should probably stick around. Arlene had allowed her children to come here because she assumed Elsie's oldest son would be available if there was a problem.

Joel mulled things over a few minutes, until his heart hardened. *This isn't my problem. Arlene should have made sure Glen was here before she allowed her kids to play on the trampoline.* He looked at his truck again. *Think I'd better head for home.* Truth was, he needed some time to unwind and didn't want to babysit a bunch of kids. *Maybe I'll go for a run or head over to one of the fitness centers that are open on Sundays.*

"Come back soon," Scott called as Joel climbed into his truck. "And don't forget to bring your harmonica next time."

Joel gave a brief wave, turned the truck around, and headed up the driveway. If he didn't hear something about Dad's will from one of his sisters soon, he'd come back and try searching for it again.

Berlin

"It was nice having you and Brian join us for church today," Elsie said as she and Doris sat at the kitchen table, drinking hot apple cider.

The men were visiting in the living room, and the girls had gone upstairs to play in Hope's room. Glen and Blaine had gone to see their girlfriends a short time ago.

Doris smiled. "We always enjoy visiting other districts on our off Sundays."

"How are you feeling today? Any nausea?" Elsie swirled the steaming cider in her mug.

"Just a bit, when I first woke up. Drinking ginger tea seems to help a lot."

"I'm glad." Elsie raised the mug to her lips and sipped her cider, inhaling the spicy aroma. "Oh, I forgot to mention—I called Joel last night and invited him and Kristi to have supper with us one night this week."

"What'd he say?" Doris gave her a curious look.

"I got his voice mail, so I left a message. I hope they can come. It will be nice to get to know Kristi better."

Doris shook her head slowly. "That's probably not going to happen."

"How come?"

"I waited on Kristi and her mother at the restaurant the other day. She informed me that she and Joel broke up."

Feeling a bit dazed by this news, Elsie placed her mug on the table. "How come?"

"Since we were in a public place, and I was

working, it didn't seem appropriate to ask for details," Doris replied. "Kristi did say I could call and she would fill me in."

"Have you done that yet?"

"No, but I plan to sometime this week."

Elsie tapped her fingers, pondering the situation. "I wouldn't be at all surprised if the breakup was Joel's fault. He can be so insensitive sometimes."

Doris's mouth twisted grimly. "I know. Just ask Anna how badly he hurt her."

Elsie stared at the table. "I hate to say this, but both Kristi and Anna are better off without him. Unless Joel gets his life straightened around, he will probably never have a happy, meaningful relationship with a woman."

Akron

Kristi breathed deeply as she jogged down the trail. She felt exhilarated whenever she ran, and today was no exception. Time and keeping busy seemed to help get her through the breakup with Joel. She hadn't forgotten about him, of course—that would take a while. But her emotions were more stable, and she didn't think about him all the time, the way she had at first. *I did the right thing,* she reminded herself once more. *Joel isn't the right man for me.*

Up ahead, Kristi spotted one of her friends from church. "Hey, Sandy," she called. "Wait for me!"

Sandy slowed to a walk until Kristi caught up; then they ran side-by-side. "Looks like I wasn't the only one needing some fresh air and exercise today." She pulled on her hairband and tightened her ponytail.

"Jogging won't be nearly as much fun once the colder winter months set in." Kristi shivered, thinking about it. "I'll probably get most of my exercise at the fitness center."

"Not to change the subject or anything," Sandy said, "but I haven't seen Joel in church with you the last few weeks. Has he been sick?"

Kristi cringed. "Guess you haven't heard. . ." She drew in a sharp breath before continuing to speak. "Joel and I aren't seeing each other anymore."

"Sorry to hear that." Sandy kept her eyes on the trail in front of her. "Any chance you might get back together?"

"No, our relationship is over." Kristi was glad her friend didn't pursue the topic. Talking about Joel made her feel worse.

Slowing her pace, Sandy glanced at her watch. "Well, it's almost four o'clock. Guess I'd better head home before Ed comes looking for me. He was watching a game on TV when I left, but he's probably getting hungry by now."

"Okay. I'll see you at church next week, if not before."

Sandy turned and headed in the direction of the parking lot, while Kristi continued down the trail. It would be getting dark soon, and she'd have to head back to her car. But for now, it felt good to run.

She'd only gone a short ways, when she came face-to-face with Joel, who'd been running in the opposite direction. "Wh–what are you doing here?" she stammered, trying to push her way past him.

Joel grasped Kristi's arm, halting her footsteps. "Please don't go. We need to talk."

As he stood beside her, she saw the longing in his eyes. *That might have worked at one time, but not anymore.* Kristi wasn't sure if her body felt hot from running or because of unexpectedly seeing Joel. *Probably both.* Shaking her arm free, she looked up at him through squinted eyes. "Did you follow me here?" Her tone was sharp, and she stepped away from him.

He shook his head vigorously. "Course not. I came here for some exercise and to wind down. How was I to know you'd be here?"

"You've been calling me nonstop, and you even went to see my dad, so I wouldn't put anything past you." Kristi's voice trembled. It was hard to look at Joel and not be reminded of what they'd once had. *So much for keeping my emotions stable.*

"I didn't follow you here. I've been in Charm most of the weekend and had no idea where you were right now." Joel slid his fingers through his scraggly beard. "Spent last night at my dad's place, in fact."

Her gaze flicked up. "Don't tell me. I'll bet you went there to look for his will. Or has it already been found?"

"No, it hasn't. That's why I decided to take charge and search for it myself." He paused. "My sisters don't understand how important it is for me to find the will. My situation is far more complicated than theirs, and they don't get how much stress I'm under right now."

"If you need money so bad, then sell your fancy Corvette."

"I can't do that. I've waited a long time to have the car of my dreams." A muscle on the side of Joel's neck quivered as he folded his arms. "I deserve my share of that inheritance."

Kristi didn't comment. What would be the point? Joel's focus was still on money. It seemed to be what drove him to do things that hurt other people. As much as it upset her to see him again, she was glad they'd crossed paths today. It was the reminder she needed that she'd done the right thing by breaking their engagement.

"I can't talk to you anymore, Joel. I need to go." Kristi turned abruptly and sprinted up the trail in the direction of the parking lot. She glanced back briefly and felt relieved that Joel wasn't following her. Maybe he'd finally realized there was no chance of them getting back together. She hoped so, anyhow.

Chapter 8

Walnut Creek

On Wednesday afternoon of the following week, Doris had just left the restaurant where she worked, when she saw Anna coming out of the bakery. She hurried her steps, hoping to catch up to her friend.

"It's good to see you, Anna. How have you been?" As Doris came alongside Anna, she gave her friend's arm a gentle squeeze.

Anna shrugged. "I'm doing okay. How about you?"

Doris smiled. "Real well. In fact, I have some *gut noochricht*."

Anna perked up. "I'm anxious to hear it. I always appreciate good news."

"I am im e familye weg."

Anna gave Doris a hug. "Congratulations. I'm happy for you. When is the baby due?"

"Not till this spring. I can hardly wait." Doris's excitement mounted. "Brian and I didn't think we could have any kinner, so this is a *wunner* to me."

"You're right, it is a miracle. I'm sure everyone in your family is happy about it."

"My sisters know, but I haven't told Joel."

Doris fidgeted with her purse strap. "In fact, I haven't seen him since our daed's funeral."

Tugging her shawl tighter around her neck, Anna leaned forward. "Speaking of your bruder, I think I may have seen Joel Sunday afternoon—or at least someone who looked like him."

Doris folded her arms over her stomach, tilting her head down, hoping to see a little bump. Her abdomen still appeared flat. Letting out a soft breath, she looked back at Anna. "Where did you see him?"

"On the road between Charm and Farmerstown. I was heading home from church in my open buggy, and the driver of the horse and buggy going in the opposite direction looked like Joel."

Doris gave her head a slight shake. "It couldn't have been him. Why would he be out riding with a horse and carriage?"

"That's what I thought, but then as I said, it may have only been someone who resembled Joel."

"Jah, it's probably how it was, all right." Doris couldn't picture her brother going anywhere with a horse and buggy when he could ride in his car. He had enjoyed driving a horse and buggy when he was young, but he'd lost interest after driving his first car during their running-around years. Besides, if it had been Joel, which wasn't likely, whose rig could he have been driving? Most likely, Anna thought the man she'd seen was Joel because he had been on her mind since the funeral.

Berlin

Doris went to the phone shack as soon as her driver dropped her off at home. After Anna had mentioned Joel this afternoon, she was even more anxious to call Kristi and find out what had caused her and Joel's breakup.

She looked in her purse for Kristi's phone number and dialed it. Doris felt a release of tension when Kristi answered, because she wasn't sure she'd be home from work by now.

"Hi, Kristi, this is Joel's sister Doris Schrock."

"It's good hearing from you. I've been wondering if you would call." Kristi's tone sounded a bit uncertain.

"I'd like to know what happened between you and my brother. Are you free to talk about it now?"

"Yes, I am. I got home from work twenty minutes ago, and except for fixing supper later, I have nothing planned for the evening. So I have plenty of time to talk."

"Okay, good. I just got home from work myself." Doris pulled out the folding chair and took a seat.

"Things were strained between me and Joel for several months," Kristi began. "He did some things he knew I wouldn't approve of and kept them from me."

Doris listened as Kristi explained about Joel's deceit and desperation for money.

"It took me a long time to realize that Joel cares more about his selfish desires than the needs of others." Kristi's voice faltered. "As difficult as it was, I couldn't go on seeing him, so I broke our engagement."

"I understand, and you did the right thing. My brother is not the same person he was when we were growing up. I don't know why he became so self-centered, but I fear he's in for a lot of problems if he doesn't get right with God and change his ways."

"I've been praying for him," Kristi said. "Not so we can get back together, because it's too late for that. I'm asking God to soften Joel's heart and open his eyes so he can see what a wonderful family he has."

"I appreciate your prayers on our and Joel's behalf." Doris sniffed. Using her sleeve, she dabbed at her tears. "I'm praying for my brother, too, and hoping someone, or something, will help him see the error of his ways."

"You might also pray that he will move on with his life and stop pressuring me to take him back." Kristi's words were rushed and sounded shaky. "I was out jogging at the park Sunday afternoon. Joel nearly bumped into me there. He denied it, of course, but I'm almost certain he followed me to the park. You know what he told me?"

"What?"

"Said he'd spent the weekend at his dad's place, looking for his will." Kristi sighed. "It saddens me to think Joel is focused so much on his need for money."

Doris's body tensed as she felt a sudden coldness. *So it could have been Joel Anna saw on Sunday. As strange as it seems, I bet he took Dad's horse and buggy out for a ride.*

She shifted the receiver to her other ear. "I appreciate you telling me all this, Kristi. I'm going to check with my sisters and see if either of them knows what Joel was up to on Sunday. It's not good for him to rummage through things in Dad's house if none of us are there. Joel might throw something out that's important or meaningful to one of us."

Charm

When Elsie arrived at her dad's place the following day, she was surprised to discover her sisters' rigs already there. After putting her horse in the corral, she stopped at her buggy and pulled out a cardboard box. Shivering against the chill in the air, she hurried for the house.

"I'm either late or you two are early," she said when she entered the living room where Arlene and Doris sat on the sofa, going through some paperwork.

Doris looked up at her and smiled. "I think we're early."

"I don't suppose you've found Dad's will." Elsie clicked her tongue. "But then if you had, you'd both have probably been waiting for me on the porch, excited to share the news."

"No will yet, and I'm beginning to think we'll never find it." Arlene held up some of the papers in her lap. "All we've come across so far in the boxes we found in the downstairs spare bedroom are receipts from things Dad ordered a long time ago."

Elsie groaned, shifting the box she held for a better grip. "I don't understand why he kept so many unnecessary things." She set the box on the floor and went to the coat rack to hang her purse, shawl, and outer bonnet. "I can understand why Dad would keep receipts from recent purchases, but to hang on to old paperwork doesn't make sense."

Doris flicked her hand in front of her nose, as if to rid the room of a bad odor. "You know Dad. He thought he had to keep nearly everything."

"We can complain about it all we want, but it won't change the fact that we're stuck going through everything." Arlene grabbed another stack of papers from the box near her feet.

"True, but before I get to work, I'd better take care of the things I brought with me today." Elsie went to the kitchen and placed her box on the counter. First she removed a plastic container filled with pumpkin muffins and set it on the table. Then she checked the refrigerator to see how much food there was for Glen. She'd brought him a jar of homemade soup, which she took from the box and placed in the refrigerator. She'd also included several apples, bananas, a loaf of bread, lunchmeat, and cheese. Since Glen often ate supper at their house when he finished work for the day, he didn't need a fully stocked refrigerator or pantry. Still,

Elsie wanted to make sure her son didn't go hungry.

"I'm ready to help," Elsie announced when she returned to the living room, where her sisters sat, going through more paperwork. She grabbed a handful of papers and seated herself in the rocking chair across from them.

Sorting through their father's mound of paperwork while rocking the chair caused Elsie's eyelids to become heavy. It reminded her of when she was in school. Whenever the teacher wrote their assignments or list of spelling words on the chalkboard, the letters sometimes turned into squiggly shapes as Elsie stared at them. The next thing she knew, her body would relax and her vision fade. Then, she'd jolt her head back up, realizing she had dozed off.

"Before we get too busy, there's something I need to tell you both," Doris said. "It's about Joel."

"What's he done now?" Elsie asked, relieved she could take a short break.

"Well, as I mentioned last Sunday, Joel and Kristi broke up. I finally had a chance to call and ask her about the details."

"Now that's a surprise." Arlene frowned. "Although, with our bruder, maybe it's not. Don't forget—he broke up with Anna before he left our Amish way of life."

"True, but this time it was Joel's aldi who broke things off with him." Doris went on to share everything Kristi told her when they spoke on the phone.

"It's a shame." Arlene spoke softly. "I liked Kristi and looked forward to getting to know her better."

"Me, too," Elsie agreed.

Doris leaned slightly forward, resting her elbows on her knees. "There's more."

"More about Joel?" Arlene questioned.

"Jah. I found out from Kristi that our impulsive bruder spent the weekend at Dad's house. Did Glen say anything about this to you, Elsie?"

"No, he did not." Elsie narrowed her eyes. "But then I've only seen him briefly the last few days, when he's come to the house to meet up with his daed before the two of them went out on a job."

"Maybe Glen said something to John about Joel coming here to Dad's," Doris interjected.

Elsie compressed her lips. "If John knew about it, I'm sure he would have told me."

"We can't have Joel showing up here whenever he feels like it, going through Dad's things without our knowledge." Arlene's nose crinkled. "I wonder what rooms he looked in while he was here."

"Hard to say. Maybe Glen knows." Elsie rocked in her chair. "Next time I see him, I'll ask for details about what his uncle did during his stay."

"If he spent the night here, I wonder if he found anything interesting." Arlene rose from her seat. "Think I'll go check the upstairs bedrooms to see if anything looks disturbed." She headed for the stairs.

Elsie sorted papers quietly for a while, then glanced over at Doris and frowned. "It would be nice to work with our bruder through all of this, instead of dealing with the tension he causes." She remained quiet a few minutes, watching Doris look through more of Dad's papers. Several minutes later, she spotted Arlene coming down the stairs. "Did you notice anything out of the ordinary?"

"It looks like Joel picked his own room to sleep in, because not one box was on the bed, as it had been before. He didn't bother to make the bed, either, so I did." Arlene sighed. "Like I said before, we can't have Joel showing up here whenever he feels like it, going through Dad's things without our knowledge."

"But isn't that what we're doing?" Doris spoke up. "Joel has no idea we're here now or what rooms and boxes we've gone through so far."

Elsie put her hands on her hips. "That's different. Joel knew we were going to be looking for Dad's will. He's just too impatient to wait for it to be found. I think I'm going to call him this evening and let him know we don't appreciate him spending the weekend here without our knowledge."

Arlene held up her hand. "Why don't you let me call Joel? I was going to anyway to invite him to Scott's birthday party next Friday evening."

Elsie clutched the piece of paper she held with such tightness, it began to crinkle in her palms. "I don't see why Joel has to be included. He's never cared to come around and take part in family functions unless he wanted something."

"Elsie's right," Doris agreed. "Besides, I doubt he would come."

Arlene's hands formed into a steeple. "I'm hoping and praying he does, because for whatever reason, Scott has taken a liking to his uncle Joel."

Elsie leaned back in her chair and tried to relax. She hoped if Joel did come to Scott's party, he wouldn't mention the will or say anything upsetting to anyone there.

Chapter 9

Farmerstown

Is Uncle Joel comin' tonight?" Scott asked when he entered the kitchen, where Arlene was mashing potatoes.

"I invited him, Son, but please don't get your hopes up." She sighed deeply, turning toward him as she placed the potato masher down. "My bruder has his own business, and he may be too busy to come." Arlene figured even if Joel wasn't busy, he wouldn't come, but she chose not to say so to Scott.

The boy's lower lip protruded. "I hope he comes, 'cause the party's gonna be fun, and Uncle Joel needs to laugh."

"We all need to laugh more." She tapped his shoulder before adding more butter to the potatoes. "Now go get washed up. We'll be eating as soon as the rest of our family gets here."

As Scott headed down the hall, Arlene went to the dining room, where her daughters were setting the table.

Guests began to arrive for Scott's birthday party a short time later. First Doris and Brian, followed by Elsie, John, and their family. The only one missing was Joel.

After everyone gathered at the table, all heads bowed for silent prayer. Then the food was passed from one person to the next, until everything had made it around.

"Ya know what?" Doug looked over at his mother. "I miss Aunt Verna. Sure wish she and Uncle Lester coulda stayed here longer."

Arlene nodded. "I miss her, too, but she and Uncle Lester needed to get back to their home in Burton."

"Aunt Verna reminds me of Grandpa, with all the funny things she says and does." Doug passed the salad bowl to Martha. "Remember when she put that wild red bird in her cage and was showing it off?"

"But she let it go," Scott reminded his brother.

"Too bad Uncle Lester and Aunt Verna couldn't be here for the party this evening," Hope chimed in.

Arlene had to agree with her daughter, for she wished it, too. When her aunt and uncle visited their family, it was like having her dad there in some ways.

Conversation continued around the table as they began to eat their meal of baked chicken, mashed potatoes, tossed green salad, and creamed corn. It did Arlene's heart good to see their smiles and hear the happy banter. Everyone had been so somber since Dad passed away.

I wish he was with us tonight, she thought. Some of the stories her dad used to share about his childhood had always brought a round of laughter. *Maybe he's peeking down from heaven and celebrating Scott's ninth birthday with us tonight.*

Akron

Joel's day had been busy and gone longer than he'd hoped. He had meant to finish working sooner, but here it was, evening already. He dashed into his mobile home, took off his work jacket, and tossed it on the couch. Then he headed down the hall to take a shower. He'd worked on the remodel of a house an hour north of Akron today and gotten caught in traffic on the way home. He didn't want to disappoint Scott by not showing up at his party but was sure he'd already missed the meal.

Better late than never, he told himself. *With any luck I'll get there in time for cake and ice cream.*

He reflected on the invitation he'd received from Arlene when she'd called a few days ago and left a message. In addition to inviting Joel to Scott's party, she'd made it clear she didn't want him looking for Dad's will unless one of the sisters was with him. This didn't set well with Joel, but he wouldn't bring it up this evening. No point spoiling Scott's party.

Joel slapped the side of his head. "Oh, great. I don't even have a gift for the boy." It wouldn't look good for him to show up at the party without a present. He had a certain fondness for the kid, probably because Scott reminded Joel of himself at that age—adventuresome, full of life, and equally full of questions.

He removed his dirty shirt and stared at his reflection in the mirror, rubbing the prickly stubble on his face. He needed a shave but didn't have time for that right now. *Just a quick shower, change, and I'll be out the door. Still, wish I had something to give the boy.*

Joel's stomach growled loudly, which only magnified his hunger. Bananas and a pear were in a bowl in the kitchen. He might have to eat the fruit as he drove to Charm, since he'd be too late for the home-cooked meal he could have had at Arlene's with his family.

An idea popped into Joel's head, and he forgot about his hunger for the moment. He did have something Scott might like for his birthday.

Farmerstown

Arlene had no more than placed Scott's cake on the table when a knock sounded on the door.

"I'll get it." Larry pushed back his chair and hurried from the room. When he returned, Joel was with him, holding a banana peel and a pear core.

"Sorry I'm late. I had to work later than I hoped, and traffic was bad, but I wanted to wish Scott a happy birthday and give him this." Joel fumbled with his garbage, while he tried to reach in his jacket pocket.

Arlene noticed his dilemma and stepped up to him. "I'll throw that away for you." She took the banana peel and what was left of the pear, and handed him a napkin to wipe his hands.

"Sorry about the mess. Since I was running late, the fruit ended up being my dinner, which I ate on the drive down here."

"There's some leftover chicken in the refrigerator. You're welcome to eat some of that," she offered.

"Sounds good." Joel gave her a sheepish grin.

"I'll fix you a plate after I've served the cake."

"No hurry." Joel wiped his hands on the napkin, handed it back to Arlene, then slipped his hands into his pockets and withdrew a harmonica, which he gave to Scott.

The boy's eyes widened, and his lips curved into a huge smile. "Wow! Is this your mouth harp, Uncle Joel?"

Joel nodded. "Well, one of 'em anyway. I have a few, in different keys. The one I'm giving you is in the key of G. I chose it because a lot of songs are played in that key."

Scott's face beamed as he held the harmonica as though it were a piece of gold. "Will ya teach me how to play it, Uncle Joel? Will ya show me what to do right now?"

"Don't you think you oughta blow out your candles and eat some of your birthday cake first?"

"Your uncle is right." Arlene pushed the cake plate closer to Scott. "After we've had cake and ice cream, we'll let you open your gifts, and then Uncle Joel can give you a lesson on the harmonica."

Scott glanced at the others, as if to see what they thought. When everyone nodded, he smiled up at Joel. "Why don't ya take off your coat and pull up a chair? I bet you haven't tasted any cake as good as my mamm makes."

Arlene waited to see what her brother had to say about that, then smiled when he said, "Well, she had a good teacher. Our mother, your sweet grandma, baked cakes so good they made your tongue beg for more." Joel reached up to his ear and gave it a couple of tugs.

Scott snickered. "Sure is good to see ya smilin', Uncle Joel. Don't it feel good to you?"

Giving a quick nod, Joel led the others in singing "Happy Birthday" to Scott.

Arlene's heart warmed. Seeing the sincerity on her brother's face brought back memories of when they were young. It was the first time in a good many years when his defenses seemed to be down. *Maybe. . .just maybe, things are looking up in this family.*

Akron

Kristi stifled a yawn as she prepared to take several of the patients their prescribed medication before they went to sleep. She'd worked a double shift again today but wondered if it had been a mistake. She would be getting up early tomorrow morning to go with her mother to another quilting class in Berlin, and she looked forward to it. But working the later shift meant she wouldn't get to bed until well past midnight. *If it weren't for me breaking things off with Joel, Mom and I probably wouldn't be taking the quilting class because I'd be spending my Saturdays with him,* Kristi thought. *So I guess at least one good thing came out of it.*

Glancing at her watch, she noticed it was only eight o'clock, so she had a few hours to go. Unintentionally, Kristi thought of Joel again. When they were dating, they often went out on Friday nights, so she rarely volunteered to work the evening shift. Those had been carefree evenings.

How could I have been so blind? she berated herself. *Joel had me fooled for a long time. I'll never allow myself to be taken in by him or any other man.*

With a shake of her head, Kristi pulled her thoughts back to the task at hand. It did no good to think about the past. She needed to focus on the needs of her patients and make sure everyone had what they needed before they went to sleep.

After she'd distributed medication to all the patients but one, Kristi remembered the new magazines she'd brought for Audrey. She hurried back to the nurse's station to grab them.

When she entered Audrey's room, she found the pleasant woman sitting in her favorite chair near the window. "Good evening. I have a few flower magazines for you." Kristi pulled them out of the plastic bag she carried and handed them to Audrey.

"Oh, how nice of you." She smiled sweetly and began to thumb through the first one. "This has some lovely flower pictures."

"I hope you enjoy them." Kristi watched as Audrey turned the pages. Then she glanced beyond her and looked at the window. Even though it was dark outside, the curtain was open.

"I have your medication for you to take now." Kristi handed Audrey a glass of water and the small paper cup with her pills. "How are you feeling this evening?"

"I'm fine." Audrey placed the magazine in her lap with the others and smiled. "Even if I wasn't, I wouldn't complain. I have much to be thankful about."

Kristi was amazed at this pleasant woman's positive attitude. She always seemed to look on the bright side of things, despite the fact that she was dying of cancer. It was hard for Kristi to understand why Audrey had refused treatment. Perhaps it was because she'd had cancer before, and it had come back. Maybe Audrey was content to live out her life with nothing but pain medication to see her through until the end. It was an individual choice, and Kristi respected that. But it hurt her to know the dear lady had no living relatives or close friends to help her through this rough time in her life. *But she has the Lord,* Kristi reminded herself. *And I will be here for her as much as I can.*

"How are you, dear?" Audrey asked after she'd taken her pills. "I've been praying for you."

"I'm doing better and appreciate your prayers." Kristi took a seat on the end of Audrey's bed. "I've been praying for Joel, too, but he's still up to his old tricks."

Audrey tipped her head, raising a quizzical brow. "Is it something you'd like to talk about?"

Kristi hesitated at first but then told Audrey how she'd met up with Joel when she'd been jogging at the park and that he'd said he had spent the weekend at his dad's house, looking for the will.

"Joel's concentration seems to be on how he can get his hands on more money, yet when he does have money, he spends it foolishly—like he did when he bought a classic car he didn't need. I think he's obsessed with it." She drew in a quick breath and released it with a huff. "Maybe my prayer for Joel will never be answered."

Audrey stood and moved slowly over to Kristi. Placing her hand on Kristi's arm, she said in a confident tone, "God always answers our prayers. Sometimes it's yes. Sometimes no. And sometimes He wants us to wait. When your faith begins to waver, dear, remember the words of Psalm 46:10: 'Be still, and know that I am God.'" She smiled pleasantly and released a soft sigh. "I am more than ready to meet the Lord."

Chapter 10

When Kristi entered her parents' house to share their Thanksgiving meal, a sense of sadness enveloped her. Joel had come here with her last year to celebrate the holiday. She wondered what he was doing right now. Had he been invited to one of his sisters' homes? Or maybe he'd gone to his friend Tom's place to eat. She was sure he wouldn't have spent the day at home alone, because Joel didn't like to cook that much.

Kristi had gone to the bank like her dad suggested, withdrawn what was left of the money, and closed her and Joel's joint account, which the bank teller said she could do. She hoped if Joel tried to take more money out, the closed account would give him another indication that their relationship was definitely over.

Up until a week ago, he had been calling and leaving Kristi messages almost every day. She hadn't heard anything from him since then and wondered if he was too busy to call or had finally figured out she wasn't going to take him back and had given up his pursuit. She hoped it was the latter, because listening to his voice messages or reading his texts was a constant reminder of her loss. It would be a lot easier to move on with her life if she didn't hear from Joel anymore.

The delicious aroma of turkey cooking drove Kristi's thoughts aside, so she hung her coat in the hall closet and made her way to the kitchen.

"Happy Thanksgiving." Kristi gave her mother a hug. "The turkey smells delicious. Is it done?"

"Yes, but I'm keeping it on low until the potatoes are cooked. Would you like to see how it looks?"

"Sure, Mom."

Her mother grabbed a potholder and opened the oven door.

Kristi stepped up to the stove as Mom slid the bird out far enough to remove the foil and expose the golden brown meat. "Yum! That looks and smells so good. As always, you've roasted a beautiful Thanksgiving turkey."

"Thanks, hon." Mom put the foil back on and slid the pan into the oven again. "I hope it tastes as good as last year's turkey."

"I'm sure it will." Kristi moved over to look at the holiday wall hanging. "Is there anything you'd like me to do?"

"Not at the moment." Mom gestured to the stove. "The veggies are cooking, the dining-room table is set, and the salad and pies are in the refrigerator, so there's not much to do until it's time to serve the meal. Would you like to sit here in the kitchen while I keep an eye on things, or visit with your dad in the living room, where he's watching TV?"

TV. Why am I not surprised? Kristi stared out the kitchen window with an unfocused gaze as she thought about Joel's Amish family. *I wonder if his sisters know how fortunate they are that their husbands don't have a television for entertainment.* Kristi didn't have anything against TV per se; she just thought for many people it was a distraction that robbed them of time they should be spending with family.

"Are you all right?" Mom placed her hand gently on Kristi's shoulder. "You didn't even respond to my question."

She turned to face her mother. "Oh, you mean about whether I want to stay here or sit and watch TV with Dad?"

Mom nodded.

"I'll stay here. You'll need my help when the potatoes are ready to be mashed."

"Okay." Mom went to the cupboard and took out two cups. "While we're waiting for the vegetables to cook, let's have a cup of tea. Would you like regular or decaf?"

"Do you have any peppermint tea?" Kristi

asked, licking her lips. She'd had some iced mint tea the day of Joel's father's funeral and enjoyed it.

"Sorry, honey. I only have black tea and a pumpkin spice blend that's decaffeinated."

"I'll try that."

After Mom poured them both a cup of tea, she took a seat at the table beside Kristi. "I'm glad you didn't have to work today, because it would have been a lonely Thanksgiving without you."

"I'm glad to be here, too." Since both sets of Kristi's grandparents lived in another state, they rarely got together for Thanksgiving and sometimes not even Christmas. Since Kristi was their only child, with the exception of some friends from church, she was all Mom and Dad really had.

She enjoyed their company—even more so since she'd broken up with Joel. Her parents had been supportive, which was what she needed, and had refrained from reminding her that Joel had been a poor choice for a husband. The only thing she didn't appreciate was when Mom hinted at Kristi becoming involved with one of the young single men from church. Kristi needed the chance to heal from the pain she felt whenever she thought about Joel's deceptions. It would be some time before she felt ready to begin a new relationship with a man.

Joel sat on the couch, staring at the TV, barely noticing the weather report on the screen. He felt miserable today—not only from the nasty cold he'd come down with, but the loneliness permeating his soul. Last year on Thanksgiving, he'd gone to Kristi's parents' house for dinner. It had been a good day, despite her mother's coolness. Joel had known from their first meeting that JoAnn Palmer didn't care much for him. She probably thought her daughter could do better than a struggling contractor. Or maybe there was something about Joel's personality JoAnn didn't like. If only there was some way he could convince Kristi to give him another chance.

Joel reached for a tissue and blew his nose. He hadn't tried calling Kristi for a week, thinking it might be good to give her a chance to cool down. Hopefully, she'd realize she missed him as much as he did her.

Remembering how Kristi had been there for him during his dad's funeral, Joel's thoughts turned in another direction. The will had still not been found, but he'd decided not to bug his sisters about it until after

Thanksgiving. Everyone had been nice to him when he'd gone to Arlene and Larry's place for Scott's birthday. Joel figured if he didn't bring up the will for a while, they might see him in a different light. He wouldn't wait forever, though, because he still needed his share of Dad's money. He also planned to talk with them about selling Dad's horses and sharing the profit. At least that would give them some money until the will was found.

Elsie had invited Joel to her house for Thanksgiving, but he didn't want to expose anyone to his cold, so he'd declined. Besides, he probably wouldn't be the best company when he felt so crummy. Scott would probably want another lesson on the harmonica, and Joel wasn't up for that.

Grunting, he pulled himself off the couch and headed for the kitchen. He felt hungry and was glad he'd bought a few frozen dinners the other day. He opened the freezer and pulled one out with turkey, dressing, and mashed potatoes. "Guess I may as well put the frozen meal in the oven now. At least I'll have a taste of turkey, even if it's not the best."

Joel ambled over to the stove and adjusted the setting. He had time to wait since the oven would take a while to preheat. In the meantime, he grabbed a tray to eat his dinner on and took it to the living room, placing it on the coffee table. Then he went to his room and got the comforter from his bed to cover up with while he watched TV and ate his meal.

"Might as well take care of myself, since my fiancée isn't around to baby me anymore." He grimaced. "I really don't like the sound of that."

Millersburg, Ohio

"Sure wish Uncle Joel woulda come for dinner today," Scott mumbled as everyone sat around Elsie's dining-room table. "The night of my party he said if I wanted to learn to play the mouth harp, I should blow and suck." He wrinkled his nose. "I've been doin' it for the last week, but still can't make *schee myusick* the way Uncle Joel can do."

"Grandpa made pretty music, too," Martha spoke up. "I liked his playing the best."

Scott frowned at his sister. "Never said I didn't like the way Grandpa played, but he never got around to teachin' me. Besides, Grandpa's not here anymore."

The room got deathly quiet, and Elsie sucked in her breath. She didn't need the reminder that her father wasn't here. This was the first Thanksgiving he hadn't shared the meal with their family. Dad's dry sense of humor and quick comebacks always kept the conversation lively.

Arlene tapped Scott's arm. "Even though your grossdaadi isn't here today, we have many good memories of him, for which we can be thankful."

"That's right," Doris agreed. "In fact, I think it would be nice if we went around the table and everyone said one thing they remembered about our daed that makes them feel thankful."

"That's a good idea," Brian said. "Who wants to go first?"

Doug's hand shot up. "I will."

Larry gave a nod. "Go ahead, Son."

"I'm thankful Grandpa let me and Scott help build the treehouse." His head dipped as he mumbled, "But I wish he hadn't died."

Elsie fought to keep her emotions under control. By the time they all said what they were thankful for concerning Dad, she'd have to pass a box of tissues around.

After the meal was over, the women and girls cleared the table, while the men discussed what board games they should get out to play after the dishes were done. Since everyone was full from the meal, they'd decided to wait awhile to eat their dessert of pumpkin and apple pies. Doris had also brought some pumpkin bread from the bakery in Walnut Creek.

Elsie stood in front of the sink, rinsing the dishes, and thought about Joel, while Arlene prepared coffee for anyone who wanted it after dinner. Elsie couldn't help wondering how Joel had spent his Thanksgiving. He'd left her a message, saying he appreciated the invitation, but wouldn't be coming to dinner because he had a cold. She figured he was probably spending Thanksgiving alone.

How sad that he messed things up between him and Kristi, Elsie thought as she ran warm water into the sink, adding some detergent. *It would have been nice if both Joel and Kristi could have joined us today. I wanted to get to know her better.*

Elsie's muscles relaxed as she submerged her hands in the water. She grabbed the sponge on the edge of the sink and scrubbed one of the plates. Most people didn't enjoy hand-washing dishes, but it felt pleasant to Elsie. The water surrounding her skin was cozy—like wrapping up in a warm blanket on a cold evening. It was one of the simple things that made her feel content.

Elsie's thoughts returned to Joel. She had

hoped her brother would change from his old ways, and maybe the family would grow, with Kristi joining them. But apparently, it wasn't meant to be.

"I should wipe down the table before we have dessert." Arlene took a clean sponge from the drawer, and reaching around Elsie, she wet it in the soapy water.

Doris picked up the dishtowel to dry the dishes Elsie had washed, but suddenly dropped it, wrapping her arms around her torso. "I–I'm not feeling well all of a sudden. I think I may have eaten too much."

"Sorry to hear that. Why don't you go lie down and let the rest of us worry about the dishes." Elsie suggested.

"I probably should." Doris started out of the room but turned back around. "Since we all put our coats on your bed, would it be okay if I went upstairs and rested in one of the kinner's rooms?"

"That's fine. You can lie on one of the girls' beds."

"Danki." Doris's face looked pale as she hurried from the room.

"I think she's been overdoing it lately," Arlene whispered to Elsie. "Even though she's only working part-time at the restaurant, it means having to be on her feet a lot."

"You're right. I hope she's able to quit working there soon." Elsie picked up her sponge and was about to wash another dish when she heard a blood-curdling scream. A few seconds later, Doug dashed into the room. "Aunt Doris fell! She's lying at the bottom of the stairs." His voice quivered. "And—and she's not moving at all."

Elsie threw the sponge and raced from the room. *Please, God, let my sister be okay.*

Wanda E. Brunstetter

New York Times, award-winning author Wanda E. Brunstetter is one of the founders of the Amish fiction genre. Wanda's ancestors were part of the Anabaptist faith, and her novels are based on personal research intended to accurately portray the Amish way of life. Her books are well-read and trusted by many Amish, who credit her for giving readers a deeper understanding of the people and their customs. When Wanda visits her Amish friends, she finds herself drawn to their peaceful lifestyle, sincerity, and close family ties. Wanda enjoys photography, ventriloquism, gardening, bird-watching, beachcombing, and spending time with her family. She and her husband, Richard, have been blessed with two grown children, six grandchildren, and two great-grandchildren.

To learn more about Wanda, visit her website at www.wandabrunstetter.com.

Jean Brunstetter

Jean Brunstetter became fascinated with the Amish when she first went to Pennsylvania to visit her father-in-law's family. Since that time, Jean has become friends with several Amish families and enjoys writing about their way of life. She also likes to put some of the simple practices followed by the Amish into her daily routine. Jean lives in Washington State with her husband, Richard Jr., and their three children, but takes every opportunity to visit Amish communities in several states. In addition to writing, Jean enjoys boating, gardening, and spending time on the beach.

The story of The Amish Millionaire
continues with...

The Divided Family
Part 5

In *The Divided Family*, while in the midst of grieving their father and settling his estate, the Byler family faces some of life's hardest challenges—sickness, disaster, and loss. When Joel should be stepping up as the man of the family, his selfish determination continues to cause chaos. Can the family pull together, or will the prodigal son defy his father's last wish and part the family for good?

Don't Miss a Single Book In This Exclusive 6-Book Serial Novel

The Amish Millionaire: Part 1–*The English Son*

The Amish Millionaire: Part 2–*The Stubborn Father*

The Amish Millionaire: Part 3–*The Betrayed Fiancée*

The Amish Millionaire: Part 4–*The Missing Will*

The Amish Millionaire: Part 5–*The Divided Family*

The Amish Millionaire: Part 6–*The Selfless Act*

AVAILABLE AT YOUR FAVORITE BOOKSTORE

Other Books by Wanda E. Brunstetter

Adult Fiction

The Prairie State Friends Series
The Decision
The Gift
The Restoration

The Half-Stitched Amish Quilting Club
The Tattered Quilt
The Healing Quilt

The Discovery Saga
Goodbye to Yesterday
The Silence of Winter
The Hope of Spring
The Pieces of Summer
A Revelation in Autumn
A Vow for Always

Kentucky Brothers Series
The Journey
The Healing
The Struggle

Brides of Lehigh Canal Series
Kelly's Chance
Betsy's Return
Sarah's Choice

Woman of Courage
The Lopsided Christmas Cake–with Jean Brunstetter

Children's Fiction

Double Trouble
What a Pair!
Bumpy Ride Ahead
Bubble Troubles
Green Fever
Humble Pie

Rachel Yoder—Always Trouble Somewhere
8-Book Series

The Wisdom of Solomon

Nonfiction

Wanda E. Brunstetter's Amish Friends Cookbook
Wanda E. Brunstetter's Amish Friends Cookbook Vol. 2
The Best of Amish Friends Cookbook Collection
Wanda E. Brunstetter's Desserts Cookbook
Wanda E. Brunstetter's Amish Christmas Cookbook
The Simple Life Devotional
A Celebration of the Simple Life Devotional
Portrait of Amish Life–with Richard Brunstetter
Simple Life Perpetual Calendar–with Richard Brunstetter

Indiana Cousins Series

A Cousin's Promise

A Cousin's Prayer

A Cousin's Challenge

Sisters of Holmes County Series

A Sister's Secret

A Sister's Test

A Sister's Hope

Brides of Webster County Series

Going Home

Dear to Me

On Her Own

Allison's Journey

Daughters of Lancaster County Series

The Storekeeper's Daughter

The Quilter's Daughter

The Bishop's Daughter

Brides of Lancaster County Series

A Merry Heart

Looking for a Miracle

Plain and Fancy

The Hope Chest

Amish White Christmas Pie

Lydia's Charm

Love Finds a Home

Love Finds a Way